A Cognac Christmas

The Brown Family Series
Book 1

LaQuarn Michaels

ISBN: 978-0-9801585-8-8

Printed and bound in the United States of America

A Cognac Christmas (The Brown Family series _ Book1)

Published by:

Transcending Works, LLC

P.O. Box 647

Lovejoy, Georgia 30250

Also by LaQuarn Michaels

The Last One

Just One More (Book 1)

Just One More (Book 2)

Tuxedo Diary (Book 1)

Tuxedo Diary (Book 2)

www.laquarnmichaels.com

Dedicated to

Z'sa, Boom and Bop

Sisters 4 Life

CONTENTS

CHAPTER 1

Cayenne Brown was pumped and ready for the three-hour trek to upstate New York. Her designer duffle was packed with all the essentials required to brace the cold. All she needed was a quick shower to wash off this morning's Spin Cycle session. She was lucky to find an available bike, as the five-thirty-AM class was jammed packed. Cayenne's mind was made up. She was ready to cheat, on her diet that is. It was no better time like the present. She would gobble down all the fixings and trimmings Christmas had to offer.

Crossing the threshold to her apartment, Cayenne shut the door and twisted the deadbolt. She stopped long enough to admire herself in the full-length mirror. She felt snatched in all the right places, knowing for sure her 30-day vegan challenge was well worth it. Cayenne committed herself to the gym five days a week, with her sights set on demolishing any pie that crossed her path. Oh yes, she was that girl who counted calories, took the steps instead of the elevator, eliminated the gluten all year long only to bust her diet wide open during the holidays.

Cayenne hoped to see her fiancé Mitch dressed and ready to hit the road. Instead, she found him sleeping statue still with both arms folded across his chest. She hated the way he slept. Only the dead slept in that position, but Mitch was comfortable that way. She called his name several times, but he didn't budge. A sudden clap of thunder rang throughout the sky. Mitch jerked forward, eyes the size of dinner plates. Those eyes switched colors, changed, and adjusted depending on his mood, the weather, even the season. This morning they were rich amber, underlining specks of gold layered in intensity. Her Mitch was always intense, on edge about one thing or another.

"What the hell was that?" Mitch asked. His chiseled chest heaved up and down.

"Wipe the slob from the side of your mouth. It was just thunder."

"Damn, that was loud."

"The meteorologist said a bad one is coming our way."

His face tightened.

"You mean your ex-lover told you we might get some bad weather and you believe it?"

Cayenne sucked her teeth.

"*C'mon* Mitch, leave well enough alone."

During one of their many break-ups to make-ups, Cayenne hooked up with the sexiest man on morning television, Aaron Phillips. Most women in New York woke up bright and early in order to see his fine ass, interpret and predict their daily forecast. Cayenne and Aaron dated for three months before Mitch caught wind and decided he wanted to reconcile. Mitch even went as far as putting a ring on her lockdown finger. That was twelve months ago, and they had yet to set a date.

Mitch swung his legs over the side of the bed and stood. Her King, was king size in every way. Her fingertips traced the curve of the intricately crafted sleigh bed. It was his idea to trash the old bed. Mitch refused to lay where another man had. She protested, told him to grow up, but he was adamant. The very essence of Aaron Phillips haunted the space he now called home. Mitch even insisted she connected with a realtor to have the apartment sold as soon as possible. He tried to convince her that it was prime real estate, and the offers would pour in. Cayenne loved Mitch, but she wasn't having it. As far as she was concerned, he would just have to work through his insecurities.

Cayenne thought about taking him beneath the sheets for one last ride but realized that would only give Mitch more excuses to stay home. He wasn't exactly thrilled about spending the Christmas Holiday with her entire family. However, he knew if Cayenne showed up alone that would only raise eyebrows. He would never put her through the scrutiny.

"Seriously though, more snow?"

"First a downpour of rain, then snow," she said straightening the sheets on the bed.

He checked his cell phone. After a few minutes of scrolling, he looked disappointed.

"This only creates more ice. Damn!"

"Welcome to New York."

"You're funny." He gave her a snide look.

"We just got slammed with twelve inches last week."

Cayenne shrugged. "It's no big deal."

"The city is barely recouping from the last hit."

The Tri-State Region was smacked with one of the worst blizzards in history. Over twenty inches was dumped on New

York alone. The intense conditions caused motorist to abandon their vehicles, and hike through the treacherous storm. Un-passable roads, transit, and air systems were all shut-down.

"The Governor needs to declare a state of emergency. It's ridiculous out there."

"I believe the Governor is doing his best considering he has no control over Mother Nature."

"He's not doing enough. I think it's safer for us to stay bunkered in."

She swatted his bare behind.

"Don't even try it. We're going to see my family. Now hurry your cute-ass up so we can fight our way out the city before it turns hectic."

Cayenne followed behind Mitch as he headed towards the bathroom. She could tell by the way he moved that his lower back was tingling. Mitch sustained a back injury one year ago when he slipped on a greasy floor while inspecting a high-end steakhouse. Needless to say, the restaurant is out of business and Mitch was paid very handsomely for his pain and suffering.

"You really should consider Yoga."

As he drained the weasel he looked back over his shoulder, grimaced.

"That's so gay."

Her mouth fell open. "Not true."

He shook the last few droplets into the commode and flushed. Mitch ran the water until it turned scorching hot, before scrubbing his hands. He knew the hotter the better. Having worked as a Food Inspector for the last ten years Mitch was always meticulous about his personal hygiene and the hygiene of those around him. He inspected restaurants for a living and still is shocked at how some people bypassed the simple pleasure of soap and water. Freshly scrubbed hands outstretched towards Cayenne. He pulled her in for a hug.

"You know I love you right?"

She looked up into those amber eyes of his, melted. "I know."

"Yoga is not a man's exercise. All that stretching, bending, squatting, downward-dog rhythmic bullshit is not for me. Put me in a gym with some weights, punching bag, and a brother like me is in heaven."

"Yoga will take the edge off, make you centered, balanced."

His kissed her forehead patted her on the butt and headed towards the kitchen.

"Who's say's I'm not centered? I'm centered." Mitch said after taking a disinfectant wipe from the pack, wiping the refrigerator handle, and then pulling it towards him. He looked in, noticed a carton of Chinese food from two nights ago.

"How many times do I need to tell you not to leave this crap in the fridge overnight?"

"What crap baby?"

"This stink ass Beef Lo Mein that's probably contaminated with Salmonella," Mitch growled.

He refused to eat out and only wished Cayenne would get on the same page. In his opinion, all restaurants were unsanitary; vermin-infested, and should never exist. Even the ones that made it past his inspection still weren't worthy of his hard-earned dollars.

Cayenne chewed on her nail. She was cold busted. Literary one day after completing the 30-day vegan challenge she'd cracked. Her cheat day was only to consist of steamed broccoli, brown rice and a side of sweet and spicy sauce. Everything changed the moment she walked into her favorite Chinese spot on the upper east side of Manhattan. Ming Lee welcomed her with a big smile. Beef Lo Mein? Ming Lee asked, and Cayenne nodded yes.

"Paranoid."

"Oh no, it's facts. If you've seen the conditions of half these *so-called* healthy upscale restaurants you love to frequent than you wouldn't be so eager to plop down at their dinner table."

"Like I said, paranoid."

"Okay Miss, I know everything."

"Seriously though, we need to get a move on. Stop messing around with the cold salmonella poisoned Beef Lo Mein and shower."

Cayenne's apartment hovered the Hudson River, stunning views of the Empire State building made living in New York that more special. Her apartment was spaciously stylish. Its modern décor had a rustic edge, simply a snapshot away from gracing the cover of some ritzy magazine. Open and airy, wall to ceiling windows exposed the big city life.

Cayenne worked as an IT Project Manager for one of the world's largest financial institutions. Her daily scheduled was demanding. With over twenty people directly reporting to her, to include managing offshore teams in Bangladesh, Venezuela, Chile, and Sweden, she still found time to exercise and cozy up to her man.

Mitch was perfectly made just for her. God had sculpted and shaped one helluva fine specimen. He understood her. Loved her, and did whatever it took to keep her happy. She felt like the luckiest girl on the planet. *I am the luckiest girl on the planet*, she thought, watching him through the glass shower door as he bathed.

Unlike Cayenne, Mitch wasn't a native New Yorker and he didn't come from a large family. It took him a long while to understand the close dynamic of Cayenne and her kinfolk. Cayenne's immediate family was comprised of a Mom and Dad who fell deeply in love in High School, was married by age nineteen and remained happily glued to one another for fifty years and counting. In addition to Cayenne, there's her brother Bay and her sister Coriander who each had approximately two children a piece. Cayenne was the baby of the bunch, and now all eyes were on her to procreate the Brown's lineage.

Mitch checked his cell phone again. Worry etched his face, then quickly relaxed when he noticed Cayenne watching him from across the room. He manufactured a smile, and blew her a kiss.

"Are you nervous?"

"That depends. How many Brown's am I dealing with this weekend?"

That question alone made her pause. She allowed his words to breathe for a second. Cayenne had to be careful with her response. Treading lightly would be wise, as Mitch could switch moods at the drop of a dime. He was a serious man overall, but the last few months she noticed a switch. The change was evident. He was almost a different man at times.

"Hum, well just a few."

Outside, Mitch gave Cayenne the side-eye as he loaded the last piece of luggage into the trunk. She promised it would be just a few immediate members, but Cayenne was notorious for omitting certain details. Besides, her mother Rosemary had a way of inviting the world to her shin-digs. She often turned a nice family dinner into a block party.

"Want me to drive?" She offered.

Mitch anxiously checked his cell phone. A smile crept across his face. He had a text, Cayenne assumed. His fingers moved at the speed of lightning before shoving the mobile into the breast pocket of his coat.

"You want me to drive?" She asked a second time.

"Ah, I actually forgot my scarf in the apartment. I will run and go get it."

"Don't worry about it. I packed a spare for you."

"Nah, it's my favorite plus upstate is a different animal. That wind chill is biting, downright lethal at times. Trust me, I prefer my thicker one."

Mitch hightailed it back towards their high rise building, leaping over mounds of snow. She watched through her rear-view as he rounded the corner and disappeared. He returned within five minutes tops a different man. He seemed much happier and eager to get the show on the road. She started to ask but decided to let it go. He was happy, and that was all that mattered at the moment.

"Alright, let's hit the road baby. Can't wait to see the Browns!"

She gleamed with joy, as she was always excited to see her parents. She turned up the music, latched her seatbelt. She blew him a kiss. He loved Cayenne so much, but he often wondered if he could truly keep her happy. She was an exceptional woman, and he was emotionally unavailable most of the time. She wanted to get married and expand the Brown family but he eventually needed to come clean with his wrongdoings. He had to become an open book, especially if they would ever have a chance at something real. *Let's survive this weekend, and then I'll confess* he thought easing into traffic.

CHAPTER 2

Sage Brown two stepped it from Jamaica Avenue, listening to her downloaded Blueprint 3. Feeling the vibe, feeling courageous, feeling like the world was hers. Bubble coat opened at the neck, hair slicked back with a considerable amount of JAM. Single ponytail, loose spiral curls dangled. She shook her long mane because it was all hers, all natural. Skinny jeans hugging her rump, accentuating her already perfect frame. Eskimo fur covered her ankles as she hopped over mounds of snow.

It was Christmas time in Jamaica Queens, and last week's storm put Metro New York on pause. Twelve inches blasted from the sky, causing delay and mayhem mostly in Queens, a borough known for iconic musicians and diverse cultures. Today was a new day. The city was alive. Cars whizzed up and down Liberty Boulevard as if they were in midtown Manhattan. City buses maneuvered through narrow streets, manipulating turns, squeezing pass traffic and snow piles.

Sage admired and respected the New York City bus driver. Her father Bay Brown was a dedicated transit worker. His responsibility was to get people to and from safely and on time. Dealing with the public was no easy feat and wasn't for the faintest heart. Her daddy had one year left until retirement. The whole family would celebrate with a seven day Caribbean cruise starting in Miami's Port. They would drift across the open seas to the Bahamas, St Thomas, St. Maarten and back to Miami. From there, they would spend an additional seven days beach bumming-it and enjoying life. Fourteen days of unplugging from the world, hitting the reset button and tapping into the vain of peace of mind was a requirement. Her daddy deserved it.

Horns blared in the near distance, bringing Sage back into her current reality. New Yorkers were so damn impatient. She hustled across the busy main street, still grooving and popping her fingers. The moment she made it safely onto the sidewalk she waved to a few pedestrians. Sage signaling for folks to stop for a New York minute, and pay attention to her Christmas joy. She mashed replay on her iPod. The music filled her soul. She switched from the Blue Print 3 album, suddenly feeling like she would get Rich or Die Trying. 50 banged in her ear. Her head knocked, her hips rocked, her stride confident. The only thing she was missing was a sign pointing and twirling to the nearest pizza joint.

Beep! Beep! Beep!

The sound of the horns and the thumbs up she received was fuel for her soul. She kept twirling, dancing and singing. Sage loved an audience. She was thrilled the world was watching her paint against a blank canvas and spread love amongst her city. South Jamaica Queens, where she was born and raised. Her family tree rooted and bounded in the soil of the Southside.

"Heaven or hell?"

Sage looked up, completely startled. Her eyes were bulging. Her neighbor, crazy Charles stood scratching his scruffy beard. The stench coming from the back of his throat made her nauseous. His buttery teeth and chapped lips made her sidestep to the left.

"What the fuck! You scared me."

"Keep your head on a swivel young'in. At all times, watch your ass from all angles."

"I was on point. I got my mace. I got my shank."

"Yet and still I rolled up on you. Could have choked you out," Charles barked. His breath was lethal. He rubbed his ashy hands together.

"Keep your head up. Stop with all that dancing."

Sage sucked her teeth and rolled her eyes. It would be a cold day in hell before she stopped dancing. She was born to entertain.

"You're slipping young Queen. Stay focused because the enemy is looking to snatch your pretty ass up and sell you into the trade."

"The trade? What the fuck are you talking about Charles?"

Charles giggle was rather sinister, wicked.

"Take that shit out your ear. Be on point or get yourself snatched."

Charles roamed the streets like a hobo. He was known to be gone for weeks, sometimes months at a time. She once saw him on the E train at 71st and Continental. The iron horse was packed with students, blue collar workers, white collar workers and everyone else in-between. Charles spread his newspaper, made himself a pallet and proceeded to sing "The Thrill is Gone" By B.B. King. His vocal game was on point, and could easily possess a crowd.

Ever since Sage was knee-high to a grasshopper, Charles was her biggest motivation. His voice was like velvet but layered in a necessary raspy. For as long as she could remember, pain and love vibrated from his vocal cords. Talented beyond words, however, a dream deferred. Some say it was the drugs. A blunt laced with the unknown, sprayed with something mysterious and dipped in brown liquor. Charles took that mind-altering toke over twenty-five years ago and hasn't been right since.

Sage saw Charles a few months earlier on the low east side. He stood outside of the Magic Johnson Movie Theater begging for change. According to her father, he was the man back in the day. He said Charles used to be fly. Fly meaning he had expensive threads, fine woman and a pocket full of cash on him at all times. He was a hustler of all things, and green was his favorite color.

"Heaven or hell?" Charles asked again.

Sage shrugged. Her eye began to twitch. It was a sure sign that something bad was about to happen. The last few days were magical. Watching the snow blanket the city she loved so dearly was a joy. Watching the kids from her neighborhood throw snowballs and make angels brought a smile to her face. However, she couldn't ignore that twitch. Something was cooking, and it didn't smell good. It was due season for the heat to show its face.

"What does Christmas mean to you?"

"I don't know. Cool gifts and good food I guess," Sage said rather blasé.

Charles wagged his stink-ass finger in her face.

"Wrong, it's family!"

Sage couldn't help but smile. Charles was right, family was everything especially during the holidays. She missed her grandparents dearly and looked forward to seeing them in a few hours. She would have to deal with her stank-ass-boujee cousins for a few days, but she could stomach it. Grandma Rosie sure could cook. She especially loved her collard greens, which were grown organically right there on one hundred acres of family-owned land.

Her grandparents migrated from the Carolinas to the big apple with a few dollars in their pocket. A hope, wish and a dream landed them both in 40 Projects, only for a short time though. They transitioned to a small piece of land off Sutphin Boulevard. Proud homeowners of a three bedroom, one bathroom, single family home was the Brown's badge of honor.

Her grandparents resided off Sutphin Boulevard for more than two decades before hitting the lottery big. As far as Sage knows, it was a mega ticket worth several million. Some folks whispered that the net value was over seventy million, but no one would ever truly know. With the Brown's latest financial wins, they uprooted their entire family to Roxbury, New York. On raw land, the Browns built their dream home from the ground up.

Sage loved visiting the country. Slow pace, clean air, garden fresh food and lots of land to discover. She enjoyed the tranquility of sitting in nature, sipping lemonade and watching the birds soar high.

"Hello, Earth to Sage. Are you still with me?"

She looked crazy Charles from head to toe, finding it ironic he would even dear question her mental awareness.

"Yes, of course, I'm here. I was daydreaming that's all."

Cayenne's light was beginning dim, so she pushed on, leaving crazy Charles to talk to himself. Her acceptance letter from Spelman creased and folded neatly in her back pocket. Sage walked with promise. She carried herself with conviction. She was on her way to becoming somebody. Sage always admired her aunty Cayenne and wanted to be just like her. Spelman was a way of sticking close to her auntie's alma mater. She would one day make her proud.

Starting a new chapter in her life was exciting. Where Sage was from, not many made it out of middle school. Most of her friends were on their second and third baby. No judgment or pun attended but she had all intentions on breaking the cycle.

Raggedy mouth Sonia and her sister liver-lip Kema moved up the hill, in her directions. Sonia struggled to push her baby's stroller in the snow, while Kema yapped on, speaking loudly for everyone to hear. Sage was all sorts of rambunctious. She loved to dance. She loved to sing. She loved to spread love with her artistic vibe. However, she hated a loud mouth heffa who didn't know when to pipe down.

"I can't stand that stuck up bitch," Kema said staring Sage dead on.

"For-real though... she think she better than everybody because she's got some funky ass diploma. She's still from the projects. Don't matter where that *HO* land in life, she always gone be from the hood," Sonia added bitterly, tipping the stroller slightly over a pile of snow, and shoving her way to a clear path.

"For- real though, you ain't lying," Kema agreed as if her sister said something prophetic.

Sage had a one-way ticket to Atlanta, and could not wait to bail. She spent her entire life on the Southside of Queens, so did both of her parents. Since they never made it out, she was determined to break a cycle of misfortune. Her father made good money driving buses but still couldn't afford a house. On top of that, her daddy's credit was shot. Her mother was a career student. Simone Brown had two Masters Degrees, one in Business and the other in Communications. It was because of her daddy that her mother was afforded a proper education. He begged and borrowed from the banks to make sure she went to school. She was laced with merit and degrees but hadn't been on one job interview in twenty years. Dream Deferred.

"Look at her, with her iPod stuck in her ear, acting like she don't fucking hear me. I know that bitch hear me," Kema spat.

"Hum huh, that *BITCH* hear you good. I should slap her," Sonia said.

Sage slipped her hand inside her coat, grabbed her banger. She would slice a predator open if she had to. Sage and Kema used to be best friends back in grammar school. They did everything together from dressing alike to forming dance groups, to dating the same kind of boys. Sonia on the other hand never cared for her. Her baby daddy had a thing for Sage, which automatically made Sonia hate.

Sage chose to hop over a mound of snow, and walk in the street just to avoid the drama. She knew that Sonia and Kema would take that as a sign of weakness but she didn't care. The sidewalk wasn't big enough for the three of them, plus a baby stroller. Besides, catching an assault case just hours away from going to see her grandparents would break her daddy's heart. Besides that, she was college bound. With a full-ride to Spelman, life was finally happening and she was desperate to leave the hood behind her.

"I'm from New York... New York..."

Sage sang along to Jay-Z and Alicia Keys. Her new favorite anthem on her lips, her ticket out the hood in her back pocket, and her banger still in her hand. She wasn't about to sleep on those grimy chicks. They could move on her at any second, baby stroller and all. Crazy Charles told her that she was destined for greatness, and the enemy was out to snatch her up. Crazy Charles also said to keep her head on a swivel. So she did that. Sage prayed against the drama, and did her very best to avoid the beef. All the prayers sent up to the most high didn't stop Kema from ice-grilling in her direction. Sage felt her heart pumping, her adrenalin rushing.

"*Ooh*, I wanna get at that bitch so bad." Kema could taste blood in her mouth.

"Get at that bitch another day. Let's go before I'm late for my WIC appointment."

Sage resided in a bucket of crabs, pulling and clawing at her back. To succeed meant that they failed. To soar above meant she sold out, forgot where she came from. But never that! Sage would never forget. She merely wanted something different, something greater and better. If that meant traveling state-to-state to find her truth, then so be it. She kept trucking it over the terrain, moving at a speed of elegance down 160th street. She threw up the deuces to some of the young hustlers that held post in front of the liquor store, and finger waved to a few old heads that stood outside the corner bodega.

A blue Honda came to a slow roll. She threw up the deuces, giving respect to the Dread behind the wheel. Yardi music bumped through the speakers. Weed smoke slipped from the open cracks of the vessel. She was surprised dude was even alive. Just last year, the Dread took six to the chest. Some said a vest captured the slugs, others said he ate them like a giant.

"Where 'ye fam rest at?"

"Who?"

"'Ye sister Cinnamon... where she be at?'"

Sage shrugged her shoulders. "I'm not her keeper."

"Tell her Dread lookin for er' Sen."

"Sure, if I see her. I make no promises though."

Her sister Cinnamon was a train wreck who was heavily involved in the street life. Sage chose to separate herself from her twin several years ago. Cinnamons beef had ultimately become her beef, and she refused to ruin her life for fast money. Dying her hair honey blond was a sure fire way to separate herself from a face that looked identical to hers. Her new look made it easier for folks to distinguish who was who.

Sage stepped inside the corner bodega and took a well-needed breath. Crazy Charles was right about one thing, she needed to be on point. There was too much happening too fast where she lived. A stampede of bad-ass kids blew past her, heading for the aisle where the potato chips and packaged cookies were stored.

"Papi, let me get boars head turkey, cheese, on a round bun, lettuce, tomato, mayo, mustard, salt, pepper, with a pickle on the side. Toast my bun first, and please clean off the blade before slicing my meat."

"You scared of the swine?"

Sage recognized the voice behind her but chose to ignore it. She felt his breath on her neck. Weed vapors released as each syllable fell from his fried lips. He snatched the left plug from her ear.

"Stop acting like you don't hear a nigga."

"Did I say you could put your hands on me?" She snapped.

Ra-san touched the side of her face. She slapped his hand away.

"Get your damn hands out my face."

She walked towards the rear of the store, grabbed a hot two-liter Pepsi from the shelf, some salt, and vinegar potato chips, and banana marshmallow moon pie.

"Don't be so mean."

She placed an agitated hand on her waist, poked out her curvaceous hip.

"How long for my sandwich?"

Papi held up an open hand, each finger spread apart evenly. Five minutes was too damn long. She wanted her food so that she could get as far away from him as possible. Ra-san smacked his smoker lips and made suction noises. He followed her around the small store, in and out of each aisle, slurping and sucking his big fat lips. Teasing and touching her ponytail.

"When you gone let a real nigga take you out?"

"A real nigga? Where he at? Point him out"

"You got mad jokes. For real, let me take you to City Island and show you a good time."

Sage had never been to City Island, but she always wanted to go. It was a hop skip and a jump away from her neck of the woods. Fresh seafood, a marina full of boats, homes with structural elegance and old world charm piqued her curiosity. Her mouth suddenly ready for succulent lobster, jumbo shrimp, fried scallops and bowl of New England clam chowder made her entertain his invite. She literarily had four-hours before she would climb into the back of her daddy's old station wagon and head upstate to her grandparent's house for the holidays.

"Your baby momma wouldn't appreciate that now would she?"

"What she doesn't know won't hurt her."

Sage shook her head and laughed. It was that kind of backward thinking that deterred her from giving locals any rhythm. He was the reason why she never dated in the hood. She refused to give up her cookies to a 40 thug. The majority of them were up to no good. Grant it, there was a small percentage of eligible young men that Sage had her eye on. They came and went daily, appearing focused and goal drive. They were obviously fighting to make it out. Unfortunately, they never noticed that she was on the same trajectory.

"You're such a Ho Ra-san."

"Not true. I just have a large appetite."

"You shouldn't eat off of just any menu."

"You're funny."

"Thought you and raggedy mouth Sonia...Oops, I mean Sonia was working things out."

"Who told you some shit like that?"

"Street's talk."

"Yeah, well that's not the case. I take care of my shorty and that's it."

"Yeah right, tell me anything."

"Stop playing and let me take you out for a decent meal, and not this bullshit sandwich. No strings attached. I promise not to..."

She cut him off.

"The answer was no yesterday. It's no today, and it will be no tomorrow. Besides that, I know my sister Cinnamon wouldn't appreciate us fooling around."

"Me and Cinnamon get bread together. That's it."

Sage twisted her lips.

"For-real, it's not even like that. Cinnamon is my home-girl. My sister from another mother."

Sage believed him. She knew Cinnamon liked girls anyway.

"Boy stop," she knocked his hand away.

"I'm persistent."

"You're a bug, damn near infestation."

"Fuck that's supposed to mean?"

She heard about him. He was burning females in the worst way. Sonia was looking frail these days and lord knows how many Brooklyn dudes she ran through. She had no time in becoming a carrier so she took a vow of celibacy. Gambling with her life was not an option.

"Nothing, I'm good though. Papi, how long for my sandwich?"

Ra-san stuck his hand down the center of his designer jeans and pulled a wad of cash out. Sage frowned at the twenty he slapped against the counter right next to her sandwich.

"Allow me."

"No thanks. I'm good. Keep that for your baby momma," She said handing over the exact change for her meal.

She grabbed her things and headed for the door. Her face lit up when she saw her sister Cinnamon pulling up in her new Charger. Black on black, chrome rims, system bumping. She could hardly contain herself. Her daddy recently kicked Cinnamon out because of her street affiliation. Her father felt it was best that Cinnamon kept her distance from the family as a precaution.

"Hey Sis, what's good?"

"Life is good. Check out my new whip," Cinnamon beamed.

"Damn, this is nice."

"I heard you got into Spelman. Congratulations!"

"Who told you?"

"Mommy. I saw her last week when I stopped in to give her some money."

"You know if daddy finds out…"

Cinnamon held up her hand.

"That's between me and mommy. Besides, they need help."

Her eyes hit the pavement. She suddenly felt bad for wanting to leave home so badly. As usual Cinnamon read her thoughts. She pulled Sage into her chest and hugged her sister tightly. Cinnamon noticed Ra-san watching.

"What up Boi-Boi?"

"Trying to take your sister to City Island but she stay frunting."

"Fuck-outta-here Ra-san. Sage is too good for you. Besides, I got wheels now. I can take her!"

Both sisters giggled as they watched Ra-san walk away.

"Stay away from him. He got a dirty dick," Cinnamon said with a cold look on her face.

"Trust me. I heard about that fool. He could never!"

"Good."

"We're heading upstate in just a few to visit granny and grandpa. You should come."

"Nah, I got shit to do. Besides, daddy made it perfectly clear that I should stay away."

"He didn't mean it. Plus, you can't leave me to deal with your bougi ass cousins. I need you sister, besides it's the holidays. We always spend Christmas together." Sage pouted.

"Nah. Bring me back some of Grandma Rosie's cobbler and sweet potato pie."

Cinnamon pulled a band of cash out and pealed a few Benjamin's back.

"Here, take this just in case daddy's old ass station wagon breakdown on the expressway."

"A thousand dollars?"

Cinnamon shrugged. She was obviously getting money now. New cars, new clothes and wads of cash were sure signs that her sister was in deep.

"*C'mon* don't look at me like that. It's all good."

"Sis, I'm a bit concerned. Don't blame me for caring."

"I know, but I got this."

"The Dread was looking for you."

"Word, when?"

Sage eye started to twitch again. It was never a good sign. Something foul was always to follow. She could feel it in her bones.

"About twenty minutes ago. You work for him now?"

"Nah, more like partners. I'm independent. I'm a sole proprietor."

Sage twisted her lips. "Oh really! So you like a boss now?"

"El Jefe here."

"Okay Boss Lady, where do you be at? I don't see you around the way anymore?"

"Expansion baby, Harlem action, upper eastside and lower eastside action. Shit, I've even branched into Jersey, Philly sector. I'm grinding."

Seconds after claiming her title the Dread pulled up mad as hell. He hopped out, holding a gun, speaking a heavy yardi language too complex to interpret. His body language downright threatening, his eyes fire red. Everyone on the block scattered. Papi locked the doors to the bodega, protecting everyone within and keeping the ruckus out.

"Where's me gwop?"

Before Cinnamon could respond the Dread lifted his arm, and pointed his tool directly at her.

"Where's me fucking money?"

Cinnamon stepped in front of Sage, shielding her from what's to come.

"*Yo,* chill the fuck out. Why you upping guns on me?"

"Me want me blood clot money!"

Time stood still. Life froze. Just when Cinnamon thought shit could get no worse the reaper showed up. Evil lurked Sage's mind all day long. She now stood face to face with Satan.

Before the Dread could take another step forward, Ra-San appeared brandishing a sawed-off.

CHAPTER 3

A thunderous applause ignited the moment Coriander Brown entered the room. Cell phones appeared, capturing still frames and live footage as she took her sweet time meandering about the crowd. Two hours late to her own event and she could care less who had a problem with it. It was her night, her show. A ballroom full of bloodsucking corporate terrorist offered manufactured smiles and well wishes, but they secretly despised her success.

Poor little ghetto girl from the South-Side of Queens had a dream to one day own and operate a multi-million dollar clothing line. Her wild thoughts to promote diversified cultural fashions, and break racial barriers by way of a single thread and a needle had taken her from the Projects to Paris.

Some called her an overnight success, but Coriander had the battle scars to prove differently. Unlike her counterparts, releasing a sex tape was never an option. Joining a ratchet television show that exposed a culture from which she was born into and loved deeply was downright blasphemy. Critics hovered and stalked, forming an opinion from the outside looking in. They swore she popped up on the scene from nowhere and made a killing. Very few knew her journey, and even less was able to retrace and connect the dots. The battles she fought left her hands stained in red. Sacrificial lambs slaughtered so that this night could one day be.

"Congratulations darling. Have your people call my people."

"Your Legacy line is giving me life."

"We met in Morocco last year at your lingerie launch. Magnificent."

"I'm a freelance writer, specializing in all things YOU. Here's my card. Call me when you're ready to start your memoirs."

Coriander studied the phony, analyzed the fake and she capitalized on those who talked way too much. She kept a fined tuned ear to the yammering of those who suffered from narcissism. With the exception of a handful, the room of attendees had a bad case of it.

"The Isle of Capri is beautiful this time of year. The Jet is loaded, baby."

"Darling, you must join me on my yacht. We're sailing to Tuscany. I have an organic winery there."

She felt a strong arm loop around her waist. Sensual, woodsy, spiced vanilla notes permeated from his Tux as he leaned in to whisper. His lips deliberately grazed her earlobe.

"His wine is shit in a bottle. You're needed at the podium in five."

The latest member of her security detail had risen up the ranks rather quickly. He guarded her every asset, in and out of the sheets. Until recently, their love was deeply coded, downright cryptic. Coriander tried best to keep a low profile, as she had been rumored to lay with the help from time to time. They were merely boy toys at the very least, but the power that grasped her snatched waistline was no boy. He was mature, developed and he hungered for her as she hungered for him.

As his arm slipped away from her frame, her lady parts went into an overactive twitch. Coriander couldn't believe what was happening. She kept her cool, tried not to seem flustered in front of her guest but that man did remarkable things to her body. Six months of face-to-face fucking, spooning and now obvious public displays of affection was beginning to be way too much for her. She made a mental note to speak with him about this.

Corianders side gaze peripheral scoped out her daughters Kosha and Saffron watching her like a hawk. Her daughters didn't approve of her latest conquest. They were both extremely vocal on how inappropriate and legally damaging to the company her actions were. Coriander considered their feelings, but at the end of the day, she would knock-boots with whomever she chose.

Coriander approached the podium, holding a glass of Champagne, her speech already prepped onto the teleprompter. A sea full of tuxedos and extravagant gowns made her feel like she was at the Oscars. *And the winner goes to* Coriander Brown! She smiled wide, living in the moment but downplaying her excitement all at the same time. Coriander knew the vultures were in attendance seeking an opportunity to feast.

"Damn Y'all look good tonight."

Laughter erupted, blended with applause and two-finger whistles.

Coriander stood statue-still for a few moments, trying to find the words. It had been a long time coming. Twenty-five years in the making and she had finally arrived. She clawed her way out the belly of the beast to now being in a room full of trust fund babies. The irony made her chuckle. The voice in her ear chimed in several times, attempting to draw her attention towards the teleprompter. The voice repeated for her to stick to the script. She removed the tiny earbud, dropping it into the bottom of her drink. Kim, her assistant looked nervous as she knew Coriander was about to go rogue.

"I've spent the last twenty-five years establishing, growing and expanding my brand. Troos Couture has been my baby. Who would have ever thought a tee-shirt hustle could grow into a global machine."

A thunderous applause erupted.

"To my team, family and friends thank you for supporting my vision. To the room full of savvy business investors and creative entrepreneurs, thank you for keeping me on my toes. It's because of you I grind harder. Kosha, Saffron, my two beautiful daughters I do this for you. And finally, I offer this toast to the little girl who dears to dream of a brighter tomorrow.

The room applauded.

"This entire experience has been extremely humbling. With that said, it's time that I step down and start planning for the next chapter of my life. Let's celebrate living our best life, and fucking awesome new beginnings. Wishing you all a Merry Christmas!"

Murmurs erupted throughout. Confusion rested on the face of investors. Kim's mouth fell open, as did the rest of the team. Kosha and Saffron looked at each other, clinking Champagne classes and silently welcoming the backbiting to begin.

It was no secret Kosha felt entitled to the throne. She was extremely vocal about her expectations to own the company when her mother stepped down. She was the oldest, more civilized of the sisters. She graduated at the top of her class from Harvard Business School. Kosha was already successfully managing the e-commerce side of Troos. Online retail sales showed a favorable forty percent bump just in the first quarter of her taking a seat at the table. She hustled hard, partnering with lead executives in the marketing and sales divisions. Together they created a fresh new look while maintaining her mother's vision. Kosha was a solid business woman in the making. At just twenty-five, she was without a shadow of a doubt a true asset to the business.

Saffron was a party girl. She was online famous. Her following was somewhere north of one hundred million and counting. Her mother was a mogul, and she capitalized off the family name. There was no shame in her game, she was a Brown. Her mother came from the streets. She clawed her way to the top and the hood showed Saffron love because of it. Although she had very little knowledge to run and maintain a conglomerate, she too felt entitled to hold down the spot as Boss.

Saffron had enough sense to know you hired the best-qualified people, who specialized in a certain field, to own and manage a process. With all the moving parts in place, Saffron would be unstoppable. So what, she didn't have the degrees and accolades trailing behind her Rapunzel wig. However, she kept her ear to the streets. Market Intel straight from the consumer was more profitable than some damn business degree.

Coriander exited the stage, stopping long enough for optics. The annual Christmas party at the Plaza had suddenly turned into a media circus. Reporters jumped at the opportunity to get an exclusive, but security wouldn't let the pack of wolves within five feet of the queen. A path was cleared for Coriander and her daughters to be whisked away into a Rose Royce Phantom that was on standby.

Inside the Phantom, the curtains were pulled closed for immediate privacy. The ladies sat quietly waiting for their mother to speak. Coriander said nothing; as she was too busy checking her newsfeed. The news of her stepping down was trending, and every media outlet wanted an exclusive.

Kosha couldn't contain herself any longer.

"Mother, what's going on? Are you sick?"

Coriander looked up from her phone, smiled. Kosha was teary-eyed and she looked legitimately concerned for her well being.

"Shaking things up."

Saffron reached for the champagne, poured a glass.

"Hell yeah! It's about time."

"Don't you think you've had enough?"

"Mind your damn business Kosha."

"That's all you do is drink. Damn!"

"AND?"

"Get your daughter before I..."

"Before you what Kosha?"

"You must not remember what happened the last time."

"*C'mon,* that's enough," Coriander said snatching the glass away from Saffron.

"But Ma' that's not even fair. She started it."

"Your sister is right. You're doing way too much for my comfort. Reporters caught you stumbling out the club white-girl-wasted last week. That kind of behavior is bad for business. *My business!*"

Coriander slid her phone into the side pocket of her designer purse and took several deep breaths. Her driver was new, well-vetted but still, his loyalty remained under severe scrutiny until further notice. She held her tongue until they made it to the clear-port.

As the Learjet pulled away from the gate, Coriander wasted no time in busting open a bag of green. Her joints were already nicely twisted. She took a long pull, held it and released. Kosha sat on one end of the plane bouncing her agitated leg. Her arms were folded, waiting for her mommy dearest to speak. Saffron sat on the other end of the Jet, taking selfies. The world wanted to know if she would be the one to step in and take over the throne. She assured her minions that she was seriously under consideration.

"You two, need to get a grip. We're forty-five minutes out from landing on Ma' and Pa's property upstate. I want complete unity amongst you two, no exceptions. My entire family will be there. I need you both on your best behavior. Be extra sweet."

"I make no promises," Saffron chuckled.

"Ma, she's out of control. When we get back to LA, she needs to go into a program."

"If I need to commit to a program, then you need to commit to getting you some dick."

"This is what I'm talking about. There's no reasoning with you. I'm trying to help you."

"*Wah, wah, wah!* All you do is complain."

"Simpleton. It's time to grow up."

"It's time you get some dick. How long has it been? Lame-ass-boring-ass-stupid-ass-bitch."

"Wow, you're super intelligent. How long did it take you to formulate that sentence? Better yet, don't answer. I would hate for you to hurt your brain."

"You girls are so damn disrespectful."

"But Ma'..."

"Shut up Kosha. Let me talk!"

"Yeah, shut up Kosha and let her talk."

"Whoa! Did I ask for an echo?"

"Somebody needs to check her saddity ass. Kosha acts like she's the reigning champion around her. Like she's undefeated and shit. Your soft now."

"What did you just say?"

"Momma, Let's face it. You're getting soft in the head. Her trifling ass is stealing."

Coriander leaped from her plush leather seat and charged Saffron like a bull on steroids. She was five-foot-five in stature, one hundred and fifty pounds in weight and packed a mean punch. With a tightly closed fist, Coriander lumped Saffron's meat.

"Momma, stop!"

Kosha screamed at the top of her lungs, jumping between the two. Coriander surrendered her rage, realizing they were forty-thousand-feet in the air. Saffron's tone of voice was too abrasive, overly thorny for her liking. Where Coriander was from, talking with too much bass and constant hand movement was to be considered threatening.

"I brought you in this world and I will take you out."

Tears streamed Kosha's face. "Momma please stop!"

The pilot's voice came over the loudspeaker.

"This is your captain speaking. Please return to your seats, and properly fasten your seatbelts. We'll touch down on the Browns Estate in approximately twenty minutes. On the behalf of the flight crew, we want to welcome you to Roxbury, NY. Big thanks to Ms. Coriander Brown for keeping us black folks employed. Merry Christmas to you all. Over and out."

CHAPTER 4

Rosemary and Clifford Brown fell in love at first site. Aiken South Carolina, 1960 and the sun had just set, illuminating Rosemary's chestnut brown eyes. Clifford could barely control himself as he tried to stay cool, tipping his hat in her direction. Small town country folks talked, and nothing was kept a secret so everyone knew Clifford was smitten. Rosemary cheeks hurt from all the grinning she did. She was super cute that day. Dressed in a knee-length floral pleated shirt, pink cardigan sweater and loafers made all the boys want her. With multiple suitors, Rosemary only had eyes for Clifford.

The towns Fall Festival was an annual event that black folks attended. Longtime friends and deeply rooted families within the Aiken community joined arms and locked a seal of love around their city. Hayrides, apple bobbing, corn shucking was just a few activities that promoted unity especially during a time when bigotry was prevalent in the south.

"Remember those overalls you wore the night we met?"

"I bethca I can still fit them."

Rosemary rubbed Clifford's stomach.

"Yes of course darling."

"Ooh wee, remember that night I got a hold of my daddy's hooch?"

Rosemary gave her husband a naughty look.

"Sure do. I rocked your world."

"And you've been my world ever since."

The gigantic fireplace was blazing. Red and yellow flickers sparked nostalgic moments of their humble beginnings. Snuggled up next to her husband of over fifty years was all too surreal. Born in a shack in the early forties Rosemary wasn't raised with a silver spoon in her mouth, nor was Clifford. They lived off their land just like the rest of the families in their tiny community. They grew their own produce, made their own medicinal remedies and even knew how to hunt for their protein before winter. However, after a leisure trip to New York, Rosemary and Clifford were hooked on big city living.

As recent transplants to the big apple, they certainly faced their challenges. With very little money, and very little connections they couched surfed with friends who'd already made the journey north. The Brown's didn't stay in one spot too long, as they never wanted to be a burden. Things rapidly change when the Browns found themselves pregnant with their oldest son Bay Leaf.

The Browns, now with child, transitioned to the Southside of Queens. Their two-bedroom apartment wasn't Aiken by a long shot, but it was home. Dealing with high volume traffic, loud talking, close quarters and the taste of city water was a real adjustment. They made the best of it. Rosemary took care of little Bay Leaf full time while Clifford picked up odd jobs to make ends meet. He worked in security, construction, auto body, however mechanical and electrical gigs were his primary source of income. Clifford was a self-taught electrician. High voltage, low voltage, fabricating, welding, soldering, and installations were a fraction of what

Clifford could do. What most people labeled un-repairable, he saw as an opportunity to fix it. Their entire apartment was designed in refurbished chic.

"Remember when I joined the association, and a few of us ladies from the building started tilling the ground and planting our seeds?"

"Ooh wee, you bet your sweet ass I remember that. Harvest time was like Christmas. Those collards, kale, mustard and cabbage got us through the winter." Clifford kissed his dear wife on the forehead.

"Rosie you've always made the best of everything. Even when we had very little."

She patted his hand.

"Christmas Eve is tomorrow, and I was at least expecting Cori and her girls to have arrived by now, since they fly private and what not."

Clifford gently thumped Rosemary's nose.

"Don't worry; the kids will be here very soon. I heard from Bay, and he and his family are in route."

"Yes, and I heard from Cayenne. She and Mitch should be on the way as well. I'm just nervous about the road conditions from last week's storm. Now we're expected to get hit with more of this northeastern madness."

"Hey, I offered to move back south but no..."

"Don't start with me."

"Okay, I won't say a word."

Silent for a few moments, enjoying the crackling of the firewood and listening to the Temptations sing Silent Night. The homemade eggnog was a perfect blend of heavy cream, spiced rum, brandy, nutmeg, and sugar. They sipped slowly. Rosemary lived and breathed for the Christmas Holiday. Saddened that she was unable to get all of her children together the last few years, but this Christmas would be different. Clifford read her thoughts.

"Don't worry Rosie, they will be here soon."

"I know, it's just that's it's been a long minute before I had all of my children and grandchildren under the same roof. I just thought by buying this gigantic house meant they would visit us more often. I had dreams of hosting big family gatherings on our property like we used to do back in the south."

"Yeah, those were the days," Clifford smiled.

"Last holiday everyone was so divided. Cayenne went to visit her boyfriend's folks in Arizona," said Rosemary.

"Bay and his family went to visit Simone's folks in New Jersey," Clifford recalled.

"Cori was very thoughtful for sending her plane to whisk us away to join her in the

Aspens last Christmas. I still can't believe how beautiful that place was," said Clifford daydreaming about the massive chateau perched on the hilltop of the Colorado Mountains.

Their daughter Cori sure knew how to splurge on the finer things in life. Mr. and Mrs. Brown weren't flashy people. Even with their hot ticketed multi-million dollar win fall several years ago, they were still low key. Their most extravagant purchase to date would have to be their property. One hundred acres of land was more than either of them could have ever imagined possible. Their home was enormous, to say the least. It was a seven-thousand-square-foot dream. Seven bedrooms, five bathrooms, a theater room, well-designed basement, gourmet kitchen, and expansive sun porch. Outside was a beautifully constructed three-hundred-sixty-degree wrap around deck to take in the panoramic views.

There were two lakes for fishing and ample space for growing. The upstate region of New York got pounded by Mother Nature every single winter. With several carefully designed and constructed grow houses; Rosemary's crops would survive the brutal climate. There were multiple rows of bountiful collards, kale, Swiss chard, mustard, brussels sprouts and buckets of garlic farm to table ready.

"You think we need to add more decorations?"

"No woman!"

"I feel like we need more lights outside."

The row of Douglas firs that lined the entryway, and led up to the main house twinkled in a million colorful lights. Black Nativity scene was perfectly placed outside, with sweet baby Jesus swaddled nicely inside the manger. The porch railing looped with garland, tied in large bows made of burlap and fresh pine cones. Matching wreaths decorated each window. Sparkling lights blanketed shrubbery.

Inside their home was a classy Christmas explosion. A beautiful custom made garland wrapped the grand staircase. Lanterns were strategically placed on every other

43

step. There were green, red and gold candles tied together with string, cinnamon sticks and winter berries. Rosemary's Christmas village consisted of intricately hand-painted porcelain houses. Her massive collection took up three six-foot long tables. Her kids often joked that she loved her porcelain village almost as much as she loved them.

Every year Clifford had the local tree trimming company enter their property and chop down a tree to grandstand. Rosemary thought Clifford's idea of having a fifteen-footer was too extravagant. However, she kept her thoughts to herself. Lord knows she didn't need that man chiming in on her village that seemed to grow by leaps and bounds.

"When the kids get here we'll add the finishing touches to the tree," said Clifford.

Both Clifford and Rosemary left a few non-essential things undone. Things like the baking, the cooking, and chopping of wood for the massive fireplace. It was important that the family joined in and participated during the season of giving. It would encourage the kids to bond and reconnect with one another.

The Browns were still strong and vibrate at their age, but there were a lot of things they could no longer do. They hired help to assist with all the decorating, tree cutting and even day-to-day operations around the property. Catherine was Rosemary's assistant. She was a shy lady who migrated from Mexico to the United States a few years back with her son Alberto and husband Ramon.

The Brown's met the family at the local Farmers Market, where they each solicited themselves as the best farm-hand, best handyman and best housekeeper in town. Clifford hired Ramon and his son Alberto to construct

Rosemary's grow-houses, and a few other larger projects on the property. The family had certainly proved themselves proficient and had an unmatched work ethic. The Brown's decided to hire the family full time.

Catherine appeared in the archway that connected to their gourmet kitchen. She stood about four-nine, box-shaped, milky skin with short curly hair. After drying her wet hands, she tossed the dishtowel over her shoulder. Catherine's smile could light up any room.

"Ms. Rosie, I go now?"

"Yes, Catherine. Thank you so much for helping me out. You're a saint."

"De Nada! Buenas noches señor y señora."

"Feliz Navidad to you and your family!"

Finally, they had the house to themselves. The Brown's tiptoed out to the backyard. Their new outdoor Jacuzzi was the best thing since sliced bread. Alberto and Ramon had certainly outdone themselves. Fresh Cedarwood, shaped into a fancy gazebo style enclosure had all the bells and whistles. The glass roof was retractable, and a well-needed feature for those romantic evenings when the weather was nice and the stars were shining brightly. The eight-seat, high-end spa had rejuvenating massagers and jets that delivered total body relief.

"Should we at least call the kids to make sure they are fine?"

"Nope, there's the cell phone. If they need us, they will call. Now try and relax."

"Okay, you're right."

It was Alberto's idea to build a sturdy support rail for stepping into the tub. Clifford got in first and then helped his wife in next. The surround sound system had Aretha Franklin's soulful voice at midlevel.

"Now this is luxury," Rosemary said sipping her spiced eggnog.

"You bet your sweet ass it is."

CHAPTER 5

As the plane came to a complete stop, a cyclone of snow surrounded the jet. The metal blades propelled and instigated the tornado-like scene. Pure white snow whipped in the air like baby powder. The door to the plane slowly opened. A gush of arctic air whistled and howled.

"You're chariot waits," one of the crew members said while guiding Coriander and her daughters safely down the steps, and quickly into an awaiting pickup. Her daddy's F350 was parked adjacent to the landing strip, with keys already in the ignition.

"Momma, are you sure you can drive this thing?" Kosha asked hopping into the front seat. She turned the heat on full blast.

"Excuse me? My daddy taught me how to drive when I was ten."

"Yes, but this is a pickup and where several miles away from the main house. The conditions out here are unforgiving."

"Stop being such a prude. If momma says she's got this, then she's got it."

"That's right, now buckle up. It's the law."

Ten minutes later the trio safely pulled into the circular driveway, parking right outside the main house. Coriander could hardly contain herself. The wind cut like blades as she ran towards her parents. A huge embrace with the people who gave her life made her sob like a two-year-old. Coriander hadn't realized just how much she actually missed them. As the three of them held on to the loving embrace, Kosha and Saffron retrieved the luggage from the truck.

"Cori, what's all the waterworks about?"

"Oh, nothing I just miss you, momma. Plus it's starting to snow, and I miss the snow. Being out in LA most of the time I forget what the four seasons feel like," Coriander said welcoming the snowflakes as they kissed her face. Her daddy wiped her tears.

"Y'all go on inside. I'll get these bags."

Coriander followed her mother into the house to find warmth. The two ladies pulled up a seat at the spacious counter. Rosemary poured them both a considerable amount of eggnog. Coriander sipped and smiled. Hands down, her mother's old fashion eggnog recipe should be bottled and sold.

For a moment neither of them said a word. Rosemary waited for her daughter to speak. Coriander always did things in her own timing without apology, which drove Rosemary crazy at times. With age, she'd grown more patient with her children. Silent tears slipped from her eyes as she swallowed a large measure of her drink.

"What's up, baby?"

"Lately, I've been feeling like I'm missing something."

"Like, what?"

"I feel incomplete."

"But why, you have the world at your fingertips."

Just as Coriander was about to explain Kosha and Saffron appeared with smiles on their faces. Rosemary hugged her granddaughters for a long while. She missed them all dearly.

"Are you girl's hungry?"

"Yes Grandma Rosie," Kosha said noticing her mother had tears in her eyes. She apologized over and over again for the part she played while in the air. She should have been the bigger person and ignored Saffron's antics. Still, Kosha refused the let the accusations of her being a thieve slide. No way in hell she would let that ride. However, for the sake of appearances and her mother's sanity she agreed to play nice with her busted ass sister.

"*Yo,* who told you to start drinking without your big Bro?!?!"

Coriander looked up from her glass. Her smile was as bright as the sun but dimmed slightly the moment she saw his wife hovering over him like a warden. She and Simone had history, and not the best of tales to tell if folks wanted to keep the peace. Coriander slid off the stool and welcomed her big bro with open arms. They've had their differences in the past, but she loved him like a fat kid loved cake. They used to be best friends until Simone captured his heart.

"I miss you Bay," Coriander said kissing her brothers cheek.

"I miss you too Cori," Bay said plucking his sister on the forehead.

"Damn Bay, that hurt." she punched his shoulder.

"Damn girl, you still throwing jabs?"

"Just like you taught me," she said looking over towards both of her daughters as a warning precaution.

"Hi Ms. Rosie," Simone said finally realizing Coriander hadn't exactly reserved a warm welcoming for her. She stepped around the dynamic duo and approached her mother-in-law.

Coriander kept a close eye on that heffa from her side peripheral. Bay nudged her shoulder, giving her that look which told her to grow up. She rolled her eyes.

Bay took Coriander by the hand and twirled her like a ballerina.

"Okay, I see you, Sis. Are you bathing in the fountain of youth?"

Before Coriander could toot her own horn, she heard Simone mumble.

"That's good money spent."

Coriander forced a smile to her face.

"Anyway, where are my nieces?"

"Sage, Cinnamon... get in here now!"

The girls appeared, seemingly unsure how to act. Bay didn't exactly know what was going on with the two of them, but something was wrong. First off, he wasn't expecting Cinnamon to be joining them. He had some harsh words for her a week before. Things turned ugly and he asked her to get out and stay out. He couldn't deal with her life choices any longer. However, seeing her piled into the backseat with her twin made him remember what this time of the year was really about.

"Hi Aunty Cori," both girls spoke in unison.

"Oh my goodness," Coriander said pulling the twins in for a group hug."

"Wow, you too look exactly alike with the exception of the hairstyles."

Simone felt her girls were already being judged by the queen almighty so she jumped in.

"It's called indi-vidu-ality," Simone said pronouncing every single syllable.

Coriander ignored the desperate attempt for attention.

"You girls are so beautiful," Rosemary said hugging on her twin babies.

"Of course, they take after us," Coriander said looking at her brother Bay who now had regret scribbled on his face. The last thing she wanted was for her brother to be uncomfortable. Besides, they had to survive each other for seventy-two hours. She pulled him close, hugged him tight and whispered, "I'm sorry. I'll behave. Promise!"

Bay twisted his lips. He obviously didn't believe a word of it. He'd heard the same promises from his wife Simone the entire trip there and five minutes into the visit she'd thrown a shot. Bay knew it was going to be a helluva weekend. He grabbed a drink and went to find his daddy-O.

Two hours later Cayenne burst through the door wearing a Santa hat, dressed in trendy white leather pants, knee-high white leather boots, sporting a waist-length shearling coat. A stampede of screaming girls pounced to their feet and charged towards the front door. Sage was on her feet first, then Kosha, next Saffron and lastly Cinnamon. The four-some had said barely two words to each other since arriving. Each held a corner of the house. It was a North, South, East and West coast beef up until their favorite Aunty arrived.

"Ain't this some shit," Coriander said while watching the situation unfold before her very eyes.

"I'm telling you," Simone chimed in.

Coriander and Simone had broken through a colossal size iceberg and agreed to be cordial. Alcohol helped the progression of peace, as the two of them now had a common irritant in the room. Cayenne was Coriander and Bay's baby sister. She was young and hip, and everyone loved her. Bay and Clifford came from the study to see what all the commotion was about. Clifford's face lit up. He was so happy to see that his baby girl had finally arrived.

"Daddy!"

"I knew it had to be you. Come, give an old man a hug."

"I miss you, daddy!"

"I miss you too. I was beginning to worry."

"Ah shucks, if it isn't daddy's little firecracker," Bay said with a smirk on his face.

Cayenne punched Bay and hugged him.

"Stop bringing up my past Bay."

"Well hello sister," Coriander said as everyone fanned out.

"Damn, that's cordial as hell. Get over here and give me a hug."

Both sisters began to weep, as it had been a least a year since they were in the same room. They talked on the phone all the time, but their schedules were so demanding it was near impossible to connect.

"Where's my future brother-in-law?" asked Bay.

"Outside wrapping up a call. You know Mitch, always working."

"I heard my name," Mitch said struggling with all of Cayenne's luggage.

"Oh my goodness, you've grown a beard," said Rosemary.

"Hello, Ms. Rosie, nice to see you. Hello, Mr. Clifford thanks for inviting me."

"Enough with the Mr. and Mrs. Where practically family now. Call us mom and dad."

Clifford's eyebrow arched, as the verdict was still out on that bozo. Mitch was playing house with his daughter, only to propose to her out of fear of losing her to another man. Clifford didn't exactly know Aaron Phillips personally, but he watched him on television in the mornings. He seemed like a fine respectable young man who obviously liked his daughter. Clifford just didn't understand what was taking Mitch so long to make his daughter an honest woman. Clifford was ready to call Mitch out the moment he walked in, but that would only embarrass his baby girl. Plus, Rosemary made him promise if he were to have the conversation, to do it in private.

Mitch scanned the room, waving hello and saying Merry Christmas to everyone. His heart lurched from his chest the moment he saw her from across the room. Impossible, he thought. This can't be, he hoped. His eyes had to be playing tricks on him, or God was definitely looking to punish him. He blinked several times, but she was there in the flesh. From the *Oh-Shit* look on her face, she too was shocked to see him there. Mitch immediately felt sick to his stomach. He knew this would be the worst weekend ever.

"Mitch, did Cayenne ever tell you how she got the nickname Firecracker?"

Everyone in the room laughed.

"Well, I just assumed it was a resemblance to her actual name. Why, is there a story behind it?"

"Follow me, brother. Let's grab a drink and I'll tell you all about it."

Mitch welcomed the sudden distraction. He had to strategize his next move. He looked over at her again. His eyes pleading with her not to whisper a word to anyone, especially Cayenne. He wanted to assume she would be discreet about their business, but one never truly could tell. They needed to talk, but how? He needed to make sure she kept her mouth shut. If Cayenne knew of the things he'd been up to she would certainly leave him for sure.

"I'm sure it's an interesting story. I'm right behind you brother."

"Bay, I told you to stop bringing up my past. I'm serious now. I ain't no killer but don't push me."

"Grandma Rosie, tell us the story on how we all got our names," Saffron asked.

Kosha and Coriander both were surprised to see she was interested in something else other than her social media "likes". Her phone was tucked away, and not in her hands. Coriander wanted to shout *hallelujah*, but she contained herself. She didn't want to make a big deal out of it and embarrass her daughter.

"You girls have heard this story a million times, but I'll be happy to tell it again."

"Yes, tell us again!"

"Well, it was the middle of September and my mother was pregnant with me. From what I'm told by my oldest sister, mother's tummy was huge. I was ready to enter the world, but mother kept telling me to hold on another day. She'd had been out in the fields collecting herbs. My little brother was sick with something awful, and mother wanted to whip up a batch of her special tonic to ease his pain. See, back in the day, we didn't have access to modern day medicines. Our pharmacy was Mother Earth. Anyway, my sister was worried, as mother had been gone for hours that particular day."

"Where was your daddy?" asked Saffron.

"It was hunting season, and daddy and his buddy's left to catch deer. He'd been gone two days already and had no idea brother was even ill. Catching deer could take a few hours if you're lucky or several days. Daddy was committed to stocking our root cellar as winter was coming."

"I couldn't imagine spending days in the wilderness hunting some animal." Saffron said with a yuck-face.

"You would if you had to," Rosemary said with a chuckle.

"You're great-grandfather was the best shot in town, but hunting wild game was very unpredictable. The stakes were high because our crops hadn't done well that year. We needed the meat."

"Mother finally appears, barely any energy left to make her way into the house. Sister said momma's basket was full of all sorts of herbs, even some she'd never seen before."

"Momma harvested the purest of pure from the fields. We barely ever got sick, and when we did there was a cure for it all. Momma stood over the old wood stove bringing a pot of water to boil. She dropped in a handful of this and a handful of that. Contractions were back to back, every two-to-three minutes. Sister suggested momma to sit, but she refused. Lastly, Momma dropped a bushel of Rosemary into the pot."

"When the tonic was complete, sister jumped into action and took over with caring for brother while momma suffered on the kitchen floor. Sister said momma's screams were heard miles away because daddy appeared out of nowhere. My daddy helped deliver me right there on the kitchen floor. They named me Rosemary because the fragrant evergreen herb calmed momma. She held a bushel of Rosemary to her face, inhaling during labor, even ate some of it."

"Here's a fun fact. For centuries Rosemary has been linked to supporting a healthy memory, alleviating pain and is generally an overall immune booster. It makes sense why granny would consume it raw while in labor. I'm sure it eased the contractions." Kosha chimed in flexing her intelligent mind.

Rosemary smiled at Kosha. She looked a lot like her older sister.

"Ironically, Bay came into this world very similar to the way I did. I went into labor while making a pot of spaghetti. Bay leaf being the last thing I remember about that afternoon before I blacked out. That blockhead boy was the hardest labor of all of my children. My second pregnancy I developed a case of irritable bowel syndrome."

"Dang momma, so I gave you IBS?" Coriander said theatrically.

The entire room erupted in laughter.

"Sure did, but it wasn't entirely your fault. I ate the worst foods I could get my hands on. I remembered a time when my momma would have digestive issues. Her system was as stubborn as a mule. Momma would add coriander to her foods and even used in a tea form. It also helped my sister with her urinary tract infections which she was prone to."

"Dang, so I cure IBS and UTI's? I'm a Five Star Chic." Coriander snapped her fingers.

Rosemary laughed until her side hurt.

"Yes baby, you're a must have. My third pregnancy with Cayenne was actually very comfortable. Bay and Cori were in school during the day, and daddy's electrical business was doing well. We had enough money to finally move out of that tiny apartment and purchase a home off Sutphin Boulevard. I was big and pregnant and happy. All was well in the world until one day I get a call that daddy fainted at work and was rushed to Jamaica Hospital."

The room fell silent as they waited for Rosemary to continue.

"Momma, you don't have to talk about this," Said Cayenne.

She patted her daughter's hand.

"Daddy had a mild stroke, his blood pressure had skyrocketed. I had no idea he was so stressed out."

"That's because I didn't want to worry you, especially while pregnant," said Clifford appearing suddenly with Bay and Mitch in tow. He leaned in and kissed her forehead, gently thumping her nose.

"What are you ladies in here talking about?" asked Bay.

"Rosemary is telling us the story on how everyone received their names," said Simone.

"The doctors sent me home with a bag full of medicine. They had me on all kinds' stuff, stuff I couldn't even pronounce. That's when your mother started whipping up dishes with the usage of cayenne pepper. Rosie heard that long-term consumption had its health benefits. By the time you were born baby, I was off all the meds one-hundred-percent, my pressure had stabilized and I had lost twenty pounds. Yeah, I was sexy."

"We named you Cayenne because you literally saved your daddy's life."

"Hence, the reason she's daddy's favorite," Coriander said winking at Bay.

"Hey now, don't start that. I have no favorites. I love you all the same."

"Sure Pops," said Bay laughing and slapping fives with Coriander.

"Don't be mad, haters."

"From there it became a tradition. Kosha, Saffron, Sage and Cinnamon, you girls will carry on our legacy I hope?"

"Yes, of course, grandma," they said in unison."

"Good. We're all highly recognized in the culinary world for adding flavor and teasing the pallet. We also possess healing powers for the mind, body, and soul. Don't you ever forget how blessed and powerful you really are."

CHAPTER 6

Bay noticed his daughters slipping out the back door, leaving the other ladies in the kitchen to finish prepping the holiday meal. It was a perfect time to have a quick chat with Cinnamon. The ride upstate was awkward, as no one wanted to rock the boat. Despite their fallout last week, Bay needed to ensure his daughter that he was happy she was there.

"Dad, we-we're just going out back for some air," said Sage.

Bay pulled Cinnamon into his arms and held onto her. She led a dangerous lifestyle, and he knew he was partly to blame. It was his responsibility to move his family out of that drug infested environment a long time ago. Tears welled up in his eyes, squeezing his daughter.

"What's up daddy?"

"I don't want to lose you."

"You won't," she said in a cracked voice.

"You need to make better decisions. I'm here for you."

"I know daddy. I will."

"Go on now with your sister, but we still need to talk about this."

"Alright, promise."

Cinnamon and Sage took shelter inside the covered gazebo. They looked around, admired the large Jacuzzi tub, plush sofas and flat screen that anchored above. Their grandparents spared no expense on tricking out their getaway retreat.

"Damn, this is fancy," Sage said.

"Yeah, gramps and granny loaded."

"Real talk, I'm scared. We almost died today," Sage confessed.

"I know."

"What the fuck happened? I thought you and the Dread were business partners?"

Cinnamon placed a finger to her lips, urging Sage to take it down a few notches. Her bottled anxiety now uncapped, and her voice pitched in fear. With every attempt to wipe away her tears, more came like a flood. She sobbed uncontrollably for a few minutes.

"It's complicated."

"Complicated? No, we almost died. That's past complicated."

Cinnamon knew there would be repercussion for cutting the Dread out the Perth Amboy deal, but never did she imagine the blowback would be potentially deadly. The Dread was ferocious in the streets, and everyone knew not to cross him. Cinnamon just figured she would make things right the moment she had business popping. Obviously, the Dread had all intentions of keeping her as his foot soldier and never his partner. Ra-San warned her things would turn ugly. He told her not to expand without the Dread co-signing it. Cinnamon pulled out a blunt and sparked it.

"Put that out."

"Nobody is coming out here. Besides, everybody drunk as hell right now."

"I'm just saying, daddy, will have a fit if he finds us out here smoking."

"Us?"

Sage extended her arm, scissoring her fingertips. Cinnamon passed the blunt to Sage who took one long pull, quickly returning it. She looked like a scared teenager secretly puffing in the back of the schoolyard after class.

"You think the Dread is dead?"

Cinnamon shrugged. "I know Ra-San saved our life. That's my nigga for real."

"I hope Ra-San is okay. Will you call to check?"

"Can't right now. I tossed the burner phone the moment we left Queens. I'm sure Ra-San did the same. Besides, he knows the drill. No communication for at least forty-eight hours."

Cinnamon took another pull, passing the blunt to Sage. She refused it.

"I'm good."

"Fuck the Dread. I've got bigger issues."

"Bigger issues like what?"

Cinnamons leg bounced rapidly, her nerves were bad.

"Look, you can't say shit to nobody. This between me and you goes no further."

Sage looked offended. "Since when do we need to make this statement?"

Sage was right. She knew her sister would take her secrets to the grave.

"Aunt Cayenne's Fiancé is my custy."

"What!"

"He's a pill head; smokes weed too but mostly call for pills."

"Are you sure?"

"Of course, I'm sure. I just served him a few hours ago outside his apartment building. He was blowing me up all morning. Texting about he's heading out of town for the weekend and he needs something to keep him leveled."

Sage stared at her sister long and hard. She was at a loss for words. She adored her aunt Cayenne, as did all the young girls in the family. They all in some way wanted to be just like her. This would crush her aunt for sure. With Cinnamon being the openly gay, high school dropout, pharmaceutical sales representative in the family, judgment would certainly be cast upon if word got out.

"What, you don't believe me?"

"I believe you, but *this* is unbelievable. This is fucking unbelievable."

Sage asked for the blunt, took a puff and passed it back.

"First The Dread, now this nigga Maverick is my Aunt's Fiancé."

"Maverick?"

"That's what he told me to call him. People on the streets don't give out their real government, especially when copping."

"This is crazy. I cannot believe this. How did you meet him?"

"I know somebody, who knew somebody that wanted to score. Told you I've expanded, got new custy's with that bread. I've been serving him for about six months now."

The sound of crunching snow beneath a heavy foot made them pause their conversation. Sage looked afraid, as they were in bear town. She'd heard stories of the wildlife wandering from their habitat onto properties in search of food. She often had dreams of being eaten by a black bear, or something creepy slithering into her bed while asleep.

"Who's out there?" Cinnamon asked rather abrasively.

Just as she was about to out the blunt on the bottom of her boot, the door to the gazebo swung open. In popped their cousins Saffron and Kosha.

"Hey, what are you ladies up to?" asked Saffron

Both bougie cousins invited themselves to the party. Cinnamon gave Sage a look, which read confusion. Their bougie cousins barely spoke two words since arriving. Now suddenly wanting to kick it made Cinnamon very suspicious of the two.

"Ooh, can I hit that?" asked Saffron.

Cinnamon looked at Sage in complete bewilderment. Was she hearing things, or did her uppity ass cousin just ask to take a drag of her weed?

"Sure, but take it easy that's some of Mexico's finest."

Saffron took a pull and smiled. It was decent, but she couldn't wait to get back to LA and score some quality, Kush. She took another pull and then attempted to pass it to Kosha.

"You know I don't smoke."

"Relax Harvard and take a pull," said Cinnamon.

Kosha examined everyone's face, and they were all high as a kite. She wondered if everyone looked at her as a prude. Did they all think that she was lame? Kosha's idea of fun was spending all day watching the stock market upticks. She took great pleasure in hanging around rich old white men at golf courses talking investments banking.

"Somebody get Harvard a glass of champagne so she can pull the stick out of her ass," Saffron giggled.

Kosha glared at her sister. She was sick and tired of her trying to show her up.

"Pass me the blunt!"

"Oh shit, it's going down," said Saffron waiting to see if her sister would actually hit it.

Kosha coughed and hacked the first few times, but became a natural after the third and fourth rotation. High as all outdoors, the ladies stripped down to their undies and climbed into the Jacuzzi. The mini bar was stocked with juice, soda, miniature vodka shots, and potato chips.

"How come we never hung out before? You know, like during the family events?" Kosha asked, munching on sour cream chips.

"Because you both are some stuck up bitches," Cinnamon blurted.

Everyone laughed.

"Guess your assessment of us is pretty accurate considering we thought you too were hood," Kosha fired back.

"True, no doubt we're hood but we're real," Cinnamon said as she held her hand out for some sour cream chips.

"I heard you got accepted into Spelman. Congratulations."

"Yes, I did. I'm excited. Thanks, Kosha!"

"I had no idea my sister was a topic at your family table. I thought folks of your caliber had better things to discuss."

Sage looked at Cinnamon hoping she would leave well enough alone. They were all finally getting along and she liked it. Cinnamon was known to wreck a good party, and she would hate for her to ruin the progress they've made thus far. Both Cinnamon and Kosha clearly had strong personalities, and only time would tell if a collision was in the works.

"Not the main topic, but Uncle Bay's kids often came up at the dinner table. I have to say, you'll are quite the entertaining bunch," Kosha said crunching on chips.

"Hey, well you know we keep it popping. There's never a dull moment."

Kosha looked as if she wanted to say something challenging, borderline offensive. Saffron knew her sister all too well. Her vernacular was sharp and unapologetic.

Saffron had to redirect the conversation before uncle Bay's girls beat the breaks off them.

"Well, I'm just glad we had an opportunity to bond. I remember we played together as kids, but things change as you get older. We all grow, sometimes in different directions but our love should never change. This holiday will be a special one, as grandma and grandpa will have their entire family under one roof. That's what Christmas is truly all about."

Everyone looked at Saffron and laughed.

"Alright Oprah Winfrey!" said Kosha.

"Speak on it Iyanla Vanzant," Cinnamon shouted.

Sage laughed so hard she farted, "What the hell is in this weed?"

CHAPTER 7

It was a pristine Winter Wonderland. Last night's snowfall blanketed the entire property for miles with no end. The long driveway that led to the main road was covered in snow. It was a picture-perfect Christmas Eve morning, Cayenne thought as she looked out the huge window. She anticipated a day full of cooking, sharing stories, taking family photos and drinking hot cocoa and cognac.

Last night went well, at least to the best of its ability. Coriander and Simone were unusually cordial. They assisted Rosemary with the prepping of the pies, baking of the cakes and slow roasting of the meats. Her four beautiful nieces had disappeared for hours, only to return hungry and happy. Bay kept Cayenne entertained with a bottle of Hennessey while her daddy and Mitch disappeared into the basement.

Mitch seemed distracted, distant to say the least. He was rather jumpy at times, which she summed it up to just being his nerves. Mitch wasn't easily intimidated, but her daddy was a big man, with large hands and even in his old age, he was still very strong. Chopping, lifting and hauling wood kept him in shape.

The smell of fresh coffee and biscuits brought her back into the present day. Cayenne looked over at Mitch, who had the covers pulled up to his chest, sleeping like the dead. She called his name a few times but then gave up. Her daddy must have really set him straight last night, at least she'd hoped.

"Good Morning," Rosemary sang as she stirred a pot of hot grits.

"Morning Mother," Cayenne said grabbing her favorite mug from the cupboard.

"Oh wow, this is good."

"Better than those seven-dollar cups of coffee you buy at that fancy place in Manhattan?"

Her question was one-hundred-percent rhetorical. Rosemary tapped her wooden spoon against the pot. Cayenne salivated at the mouth as her mother dropped two handfuls of freshly grated smoked cheddar cheese into piping hot grits. The biscuits were buttered; the bacon crispy and the eggs were extra fluffy.

"Ooh wee, let me restrain myself before I go to work in this kitchen," said Cayenne as she sipped her perfectly roasted coffee. She had to admit, it was the best cup of Java she'd had in a very long time.

"Where is everyone?"

"Bay and Daddy outside clearing the driveway with the blower, Cori and Simone passed out sleep and the girls are too. It's just us here at the moment."

"Good, I wanted to get your opinion on something."

"Okay, what's on your mind Firecracker?"

Just as Cayenne was to unload her concerns onto her mother, the front door swung opened. In walked God's perfect creation. His body was a framework of all kinds of sexy. Never ever had she met a man on first site and wanted to fuck him. His cowboy sexy vibe was intriguing. He was dressed in a plaid flannel shirt, bubble vest, jeans, and snow-covered boots. His rugged mountain man persona had Cayenne feeling all sorts of ways.

"Good Morning Ms. Rosie. Forgive my interruption."

"Alberto, come inside. I thought we gave you the day off? What are you doing here on Christmas Eve?"

"The storm last night was pretty bad. *Muy Mal*. It knocked down several power lines. Me and Papi figured we'd come to check on you."

"Ramon is here too? But it's Christmas Eve Alberto. I feel terrible."

Alberto chuckled. "Please don't be. It's my pleasure. Besides, Mi Madra is busy with her sisters from California. They're cooking up Tamales, Pavo, Pozole, tripe soup, lamb. The list goes on. Anyway, Mr. Clifford asked that I grab the portable generator from the basement hall closet."

"That silly blower must have lost power again?"

"Yes ma'am, it did."

Alberto noticed Cayenne hiding behind the fridge door.

"Hello, I'm Alberto. You must be Cayenne. Nice to meet you?"

"How would you know that?"

"Ms. Rosie is proud of all of her children. I've also seen pictures. I feel like I know you."

"Wish I could say the same."

Cayenne did not like being caught off guard, especially when a fine ass specimen like Alberto was in her midst. Her motto was to always *Stay Ready*. Not following her own rule obviously left her looking all kinds of crazy. Her hair and makeup weren't done and she was dressed in a reindeer onesie. Rosemary provided pajamas for everyone, as she wanted a Christmas theme sleepover. Too embarrassed to look in his direction, she offered up an overzealous handshake.

"Wow, you've got a firm grip there."

"Well, my daddy always said your grip was as good as your word and it better be firm."

"Ah. Mr. Clifford is a very smart man. I admire his wisdom."

Finally, she looked up at him. His eyes were dreamy, and his hands were like butter. Her parents mentioned hiring help, but her mother failed to mention how good looking. Alberto's voice sounded exotic, downright intoxicating.

"You look even better in person," Alberto said.

"Thank you," she stammered.

Rosemary cleared her throat.

"Can I offer you to a plate of food, perhaps a cup of coffee?"

"Ma, the man just said he has a house full of food. Which sounds very delicious by the way," Cayenne added.

"No, she's right Ms. Rosie. We're here to do a job and then we must run," Alberto said flashing a smile in Cayenne's direction.

"Well alright, you know your way around this place. Go ahead and get what you need."

Cayenne watched as Alberto disappeared into the basement. She pulled up a stool, folded her arms. Rosemary buried her smirk for as long as possible. She was notorious for low key matchmaking, especially when it came to Cayenne. She was the only one without a husband or kids, and Rosemary wanted more grandbabies.

"Spill it, momma."

"What do you mean?"

Cayenne tilted her head to the left, twisted her lips.

"Okay, I kind of knew he would show. Alberto's a nice guy, plus he's handy and..."

"I'm engaged to Mitch, who by the way is right upstairs asleep," Cayenne whispered.

She wiggled her fingers, showcasing her bling.

"You know I love Mitch. I truly do look at him as my son, but that man has some serious commitment issues. If he's not ready to pull the trigger, then I'm sorry baby he's not the one for you. Also, why isn't he outside helping daddy and Bay clear the road?"

Rosemary's eyebrows rose only to silently insinuate that Mitch was lazy.

"Momma you know he hurt his back on the job last year. He needs to take it easy, doctor's orders. Besides, that's what you hired help for."

Rosemary lifted her wooden spoon and pointed towards the door.

"He had no issues dragging all your luggage up in her yesterday."

"Momma, Mitch is asleep. Let him be, please."

Cayenne cringed the moment she said it. Never did she imagine she would become that kind of woman who made excuses for her man. She had always despised those who did, as it was a sign of weakness. The fact of the matter was Mitch was stringing her along. He proposed out of fear of another man stealing his prize. She knew it and the entire family did as well.

CHAPTER 8

Clouded by the cannabis smoke, semi levitated with a taste of Hennessy on her tongue. Cinnamon woke up, only to realize she was in some far off land. A fairytale of some sort where the grass is always green, where roses bloomed and lemonade is filled to the rim of pitchers covered in sunflower decorations. For days she'd been couch surfing. Her father Bay was serious this time. He wanted several degrees of separation, for the sake of the family's well being of course. He felt endangered, and she couldn't blame him. Her name was circulating among the locals. Hood famous came with a price.

Ra-San was cool with her bunking at his mom's but things got hectic when Ms. Irene found a baggy on her bathroom floor. It certainly wasn't hers, and it damn sure wasn't Ra-sans. They were past mediocre operations. Truth be told, it was Ms. Iren's God fearing, bible toting husband getting-down-with-that-get-down. Like a Boss, Cinnamon took the wrap. Ra-san needed a roof, so it only made sense. Besides, they were still in the infancy stage of making moves. Why rock the boat?

For the first time, she noticed how beautifully decorated the room was. The customized bed was fit for a king, designed for a queen and could easily host a party of four. Her mind went someplace perverted and back. Not exactly sure how she made it to bed, but she knew for a fact that last night's Turn-Up was epic. Cinnamon couldn't wait to speak with her sister and rehash the events. Tossing her legs over the side of the bed, standing to stretch only to realize she was dressed in a reindeer onesie.

"What kind of freaky shit is going on?"

She didn't remember undressing, especially purposely putting on a onesie with antlers. Cinnamon scratched her head and wondered where her sister was. There better be a good explanation for why she looked like this. The old tree perched outside her bedroom window looked rather beautiful with its branches bare, and frozen ice sickles dripping from the morning's sun. Her stomach rumbled as she smelled food.

Cinnamon didn't bother to change. Who had time for that? She slipped on her favorite baseball cap and grabbed the doorknob. Just as the door swung opened, a large set of hands covered her mouth shoving her back inside. Her daddy made sure she was nice with the hands, but she was no match towards him. It was the second time in her life she felt overpowered by a man. The first was by a boy from her neighborhood who pinned her down on a plastic covered sofa and attempted to crack her safe.

"Shush, don't scream."

"Get the fuck off me."

"Relax, I just want to talk."

She froze for a second, recalling how that boy humped on her and tried to force his grimy hand up her denim skirt. Cinnamon remembered how hot and heavy his breathing was, and how motivated he was to take her innocents.

That day, she was merely out jumping rope with her friend Taj when Taj suddenly needed to run upstairs to her aunt's apartment to use the bathroom. Taj disappeared, and in walked her cousin with his cock out ready to violate her. It was a quiet struggle as if she was afraid to scream, as if she would offend him by crying foul. She squirmed, punched and kicked but never did a vocal pass her lips. Finally, he figured she wasn't putting out, so he let up. Until this day she questioned if Taj set her up to be raped.

Suddenly back to the future, she noticed that Mitch had all kinds of crazy in his eyes. Cinnamon looked around for something to grab and defend herself with. Everything was soft and fluffy and possessed no real mass. With all her might and with everything her daddy taught her she started to wild-out. Still silent in her rage, she kicked and punched her way free.

"Okay, stop I didn't mean any harm. I just want to talk."

"I know what kind of talking you want to do."

Both hands raised in a surrendering fashion.

"See, it's not like that. I'm a peaceful brother."

With no real plan in place to confront her, Mitch chose intimidation as the first options. She obviously wasn't having it, so he piped down and chose to revert to a more civilized matter.

"Look, I didn't mean to come off creepy. I just want to talk."

"Fuck me is all. You think I'm stupid?"

"Listen, that's not even the case. I'm just looking to come to some sort of agreement. You know, be on the same page."

Mitch urged Cinnamon to have a seat, but she refused. He paced the room realizing he'd made matters worse. He was no threat. He would never sexually assault anyone. Never in a million years did he ever see himself in this state of affairs, and looked on as some vile rapist. He needed to contain the situation. He stopped pacing and quickly locked the bedroom door.

Cinnamon sucked back air. Fear danced in her eyes, but she remained un-flinched. Across the room was a glass bowl decorated with angels. If only she could get to it. He moved in close, and she took several steps back.

"I'm not going to hurt you."

"I'll scream."

"Fuck! Will you just listen to me? I'm not going to hurt you."

"What the fuck Maverick, or should I call you Mitch?"

He stopped pacing, looked up at her.

"I need you to forget we ever met," he spoke very slow and deliberate.

"She can never know."

"Yo, get the fuck out of my room."

"We're practically family, and I would hate to tell everyone all that you've been up to."

"Look man, I've got nothing to hide. You want to out me to my family? Go ahead. I welcome it. I need to atone for my sins."

"The things I know will have you in a pair of bracelets within the hour."

She sucked her teeth. "Do it."

"The things I know will disgrace your family name. You've been a bad girl, and I've got evidence to prove it."

"Motherfucker it's hard being me. You need to get some shit off your chest, by all means, there's the door." She pointed.

"You don't mean that."

"Oh, my word is my bond. Do it!"

The challenge was in the air. He wasn't dealing with some naive drug peddler who hustled for an outfit and kicks. She wasn't your average chick looking for the latest handbag, shoes and enough for a raggedy ass sew-in. Cinnamon was a Brown. She was a survivor. They were the most stubborn group of folks he'd ever met in his entire life. Once their mind was set, it was stone. There she stood in a ridiculous costume daring him to snitch. Mitch was sincerely puzzled as to why she hadn't screamed bloody murder at this point. Realizing his actions thus far would have called for those intense measures, he certainly was happy she didn't.

He started to speak, but she interrupted.

"I know too much. You want me silenced, but you ain't about that life."

He scuffed.

"You don't know what I'm capable of."

She tilted her head, finally seeing the bitch in him. He was baby soft, sweet as pie. What he didn't realize is if anything happened to her, double would happen to his family in Arizona. Mitch crossed the line the moment he put his hands on her. It was only a matter of time before she pulled the ceiling down on his head. She moved up close and personal, trigger finger to his dome. The fear that once glazed her pupils was gone. He now saw the devil in her eyes. Mitch stepped aside, permitting Cinnamon to leave.

"That's what I thought. You're a fucking a joke and my aunt can do way better."

***

After breakfast, it was time for the family portrait. Rosemary insisted that everyone sported matching Christmas sweaters. Saffron protested at first, in fear of the photo being leaked to her minions on social media. She had a reputation to uphold. It was bad enough grandma Rosie made her wear the hideous onesie, now she wanted her to smile for the cameras with some ugly Christmas sweater. Coriander threatened to cut her off financially if she didn't play nice.

Rosemary couldn't help but get emotional. She had all of her family under one roof. God was definitely good to her. Most of her friends had gone home to see the lord. Here she was in this beautiful home, with her children and her grandchildren. The lord had certainly smiled down on her.

"Momma, don't mess up your makeup," Coriander said dabbing Rosemary's cheeks.

"Can we hurry, I'm starting to get a cramp in my leg," Bay said.

"Seriously though, I'm not sure how long I can hold this pose," Cayenne chimed in.

Others started to grumble and complain of this and that, and everything in between. Grandpa Cliff whistled loudly, commanding everyone's attention. Back in the day Bay, Coriander and Cayenne would hear that same whistle from two blocks away and knew it was their daddy calling them home.

"Just a few more poses, and we can all relax."

Clifford looked over his shoulder and gave Alberto the go-ahead to continue snapping photos. Alberto insisted that he stayed on the property to ensure the Browns had whatever they needed. Of course, Rosemary protested such an idea. For heaven's sake, it was Christmas Eve. Alberto assured her it was no problem. His father Ramon was long gone, but Clifford had promised to give him a lift home whenever he was ready.

Everyone knew Alberto had eyes for Cayenne except Mitch. His mind was definitely preoccupied with other thoughts. Alberto would await the right opportunity to slip his number to Cayenne. If only he could get her alone for two seconds. He was a traditional man, and would never pursue a lady who was already taken. Alberto had morals, but something special happened to him the moment he laid eyes on Cayenne. His ethics book went out the window, and he just had to have her.

Coriander nudged Cayenne and whispered.

"Papi Chulo is looking for you to sprinkle a little Cayenne on his burrito.

"Stop it."

"On three, say Cheese!"

After several rounds of posing, smiling and holding still the Brown's broke away in search of some alcohol. Bay poured up the adults, while he eyeballed Sage and Cinnamon from across the room. He could tell by the scroll on Cinnamons face something was wrong. He thought to interject but figured he'd let the situation breathe. Whatever it was, Sage would smooth things over. She always did.

Bay directed his attention to his wife Simone who seemed tipsy. Simone had been sipping on mimosa since breakfast, and now had graduated to screwdrivers. Mixing alcohol was never wise, especially when it came to Simone. She battled sobriety for many years. Her on again, off again affair with booze almost damaged their marriage.

Things had taken a turn for the worst one year. Bay was ready to call it quits. He would often return home after a long day at work to find Simone sloppy drunk, yelling out the window at the neighborhood kids. He started to pick up extra shifts, but Simone knew better. It was a pretty young receptionist at the bus depot that had his attention. Simone did what it took to clean up her act and repair her marriage. Now, she barely touched the stuff, with the exception of holidays. Bay wished Simone would give it up altogether, but who was he to judge when he enjoyed a beer or two every day after working a long shift.

Bay worked for New York City Transit driving a bus. Survival of the fittest, and only the strong survived as he sat behind that big wheel. Every day presented a new challenge as he drove a packed bus, full of irate passengers, badass kids and a combination of offensive hygienic and ethnic odors. Bay had his share of run-ins with disrespectful teenagers, as he once got snuffed from behind, spit on and called everything but the child of God. A homeless man who refused to depart the bus at the end of his route pulled a switchblade on him. He cold clocked the man, knocking his lights out. It was self-defense and never went against his squeaky clean record. Bay was elated because this time next year, he would officially be retired.

Simone tugged at Corianders sweater and whispered something in her ear. Whatever she said clearly struck a nerve as Coriander proceeded to separate herself. A little distance would surely help the situation Bay thought as he watched from afar. Simone followed Coriander like a shark, circling her and taunting her. Simone tugged at the bottom of Corianders sweater a second time. Coriander turned on her heels, lifted her finger as if to say *don't test me*. Bay hurried to his wife's side, looping his arm around her waist. She was past tipsy, as she was now slurring her words.

"Come, baby, its way too early for this drama."

"Says who?"

Coriander headed towards the staircase, refusing to entertain her drunken sister-in-law. It was Christmas Eve, and all she wanted was some peace. She figured she would go change out of the awful sweater, into something more classy and elegant. She had to breathe deeply, as she was thoroughly annoyed. For her parent's sake, she had to remain cool. It took everything not to slap Simone stupid ass into the middle of next week. Coriander actually felt silly for avoiding the confrontation, but she had to. She was a conglomerate. A goddamn walking law-suit and she knew all too well Simone wanted a piece of her fortune.

"You're always taking up for that bitch!"

"Calm down Simone, you're embarrassing yourself."

"Oh, so I embarrass you? I'm not good enough?" She slurred and shoved Bay.

Sage and Cinnamon appeared, trying to get their mother under control.

"Oh, oh, okay. I'm not good enough for Y'all either I see. Oh, oh, okay."

"We didn't say that. Let's just go take a nap," Bay said stroking her back.

"That fucking bitch owes me big time. It was our tee-shirt business. She cut me out."

And there it was. Simone still harbored feelings from back in the day as she should. They used to be best friends, inseparable. Together they had a dream to sell their tee-shirts in the Coliseum on Jamaica Avenue, 125th street in Harlem, Fordham Road in the Bronx, and on Pickens Avenue in Brooklyn. That was the problem. Coriander saw past hood recognition. She saw her name in the lights. She saw a global enterprise. They had the power to impact real change in their community, and stimulate their local economy but Simone was allergic to the big picture.

Everyone knew Simone loved school. She was a straight-A student and labeled intellectually gifted. The library was her sanctuary. She read three books a week, in addition to keeping up with her studies. She was super bright, but all of that knowledge was useless if not applied. Simone talked a good game, but she was a serial procrastinator. She had the most amazing ideas but never made it past the brainstorming phase. Tomorrow, someday, eventually were her favorite words. Coriander grew tired of waiting. She realized their visions would never align. Their situation was getting no better. Coriander was guilty of making a mad dash, holding the bag and ultimately pulling the trigger to her own success.

"You ripped the rug from under me. You ain't shit Cori. You're nothing but a fucking snake."

"Well call me Ms. Python," Coriander bit her tongue. She told herself not to engage.

"Take off that mask cause we all know the real you. You're a fucking phony."

At this point, the entire family was watching. Her daughters looked completely mortified by the situation. Her parents shook their heads and told them both to hush up all that noise. Mitch was playing Cayenne extra close, as he noticed Alberto eye-balling her during the photo session. Bay and his daughters helplessly tried to control Simone. At this point, she was trying to fight her way up the steps to get at Coriander. Even Alberto looked on, puzzled and not knowing what to do to assist. Coriander waived her off, like *by Felicia*.

"You ran the streets whore! It was my idea. It was my research."

"Stop acting crazy," Bay gritted his teeth.

"Simone, this is not the time for this," Cayenne chimed in. Her face was tight. She didn't want to jump into the drama, but that was her sister. Regardless of good bad or indifferent, she would protect her blood. Cayenne sucked her teeth at her brother Bay. *Coward!*

"Cori you're nothing but a snake. Gold digging ass bitch!"

"It truly amazes me how you can stand there and throw stones. Yes, I've done a lot of things I'm not proud of, but that's all in the past. I'm not expecting you're over-educated, broke ass to understand any of this. I just ask that you respect my parent's home. Now I've been extremely tolerant of you, for the sake of my brother, my parents, and sweet baby Jesus. However, there's so much abuse I'm willing to accept. Now, if there's nothing further I'll be in my room changing into something a little more comfortable. Perhaps you take a nap, dry out and maybe we can continue this conversation like two grown-ass adults."

"Tolerant of me? Are you serious? You're a fucking slut. I bet you Kosha don't know who her daddy is?"

The entire room gasped. A tense silence blanketed the room. Coriander made it to the third step, clinched the iron wrought railing. Rosemary's garland was two seconds from being wrapped around that heffas throat. She swallowed hard, trying best not to disturb her mother's beautiful décor. The voice in her head told her to proceed, that she wasn't worth the fuss. It wasn't until she saw Kosha and Saffron's anxious face that she realized one her deepest darkest secrets would be revealed.

"Crazy Charles is your daddy!"

CHAPTER 9

er body became a furnace and everything turned red. Coriander leaped off the third step, slamming her fist into Bay's jaw. He quickly succumbs to the pain, as he held his face no longer able to shield his wife from Corianders wrath. Simone's eyes widened, and before she could scream for help Coriander was on top of her.

The thing about Coriander most people didn't realize was she didn't have an off switch. She was usually up or down, with no middle grown. She was often hot or cold with no space for room temperature. Easily angered would be putting it mildly. As a child, Coriander was prone to episodes of anger. The Browns couldn't afford therapy, besides black folks didn't believe in shrinks back in the day. How could someone white, understand and correctly diagnose their plight? Also, the stigma and judgment from the black community alone were certainly enough to make one avoid psychotherapy.

The Browns prayed heavily and Coriander found marijuana as a method of coping. The twisted leaf gave her balance and brought some serious calmness to her life but it was merely a Band-Aid. It wasn't until a few years ago did Coriander finally accepted she needed help. With all of her success, fame, and fortune she had to admit she was broken. Ms. Ann, her therapist was a Godsend. A lady well into her sixties, but you couldn't tell by looking at her. She had short platinum spunky hair, bedazzled goggle frames, with a yoga body to die for. If you squinted hard enough she kind of favored an older Julia Roberts.

"Stop Cori, let her go," Cayenne's voice was at a shrill.

"Cori, she can't breathe. Let her go!" Rosemary screamed.

"Aunty please, let her go. She's got asthma," Sage begged but didn't dare step in.

Her mother had it coming. She grew up hearing all kinds of filthy things about her aunt Cori, but her dealings with Crazy Charles was a first. She looked over at Kosha and instantly saw the resemblance. They had the same eyes, and nose. Her family had more secrets than a little bit, she thought now glaring at Mitch. After her sister Cinnamon told her what was up, she instantly had it out for the man. *I should throw his ass underneath the bus*, Sage thought. It was no perfect time like the present.

Mitch felt the heat on his neck from Sage. The nasty scroll on her face confirmed his fears. Cinnamon had blabbed her damn mouth. It was as if he could suddenly read Sage's thoughts. As a preventative measure, he jumped in to grab Simone from the tussle. Her legs were wobbly and were just about to give way. He helped her to a nearby seat in the foyer. It took both Clifford and Alberto to restrain Coriander. Simone massaged her throat, coughed and hacked uncontrollably for minutes. In the far left corner, Coriander was ready for round two.

"You fucking... bitch," Simone said hoarsely.

Blinded with rage Coriander bulldozed through her daddy and Alberto, and charged towards Simone. Both Cinnamon and Sage jumped up to shield their mother.

"Aunty, that's enough. I get your upset, but you've got yours off," said Cinnamon.

"Yes, please aunty. With all due respect, we can't let you hit her again."

The word *LET* sent a tinge of rage down Kosha's spine. She looked as if she wanted to say something in her mother's defense, but Saffron shook her head no. Saffron didn't want to make matters worse. Besides, their mother was from the streets. She could handle herself in this matter. They were born and raised privileged. The last thing she needed was her followers to know she'd been mopped and dragged on Christmas Eve.

"CORI!"

Coriander snapped out of the explosive trance when she heard her daddy's voice. She turned to see the painstaking looking on her parent's face. Rosemary's hands were clasped together. She had tears in her eyes. Her father pulled her into his chest. She trembled in his arms for a long while before breaking away from the embrace.

"I need some air."

"I could use some air too," said Clifford grabbing two insulated coats from the closet, and passed one to Coriander. Clifford completely forgot Alberto was still in the room. The old man was so embarrassed.

"Alberto, about that lift home?"

"No worries Mr. *C*, my father is on the way now. He's five minutes out."

"Look, son I'm sorry if we've ruined your Christmas with all the mudslinging."

"Not at all Mr. *C*. I'm Mexican, so this is another day at my house. In fact, I'm pretty sure my aunt Lucy has found the Tequila stash. She's the best mudslinger you will ever meet."

Several hours later, the Brown's home was in a semi-peaceful state. Rosemary was clearly worked up, as all the commotion brought on a serious migraine. Clifford reassured her all was well, and that she should take a nap.

Both Bay and Simone retreated to their quarters to nurse each other's wounds. The beating they took caused some serious bruising, but thankfully nothing was broken. The North, South, East and West coast beef had re-ignited once again, as the girls barely said two words after the big blow up.

Kosha's mind raced in a million different directions. This crazy Charles character presumably was her biological father. The moment his name was dropped it was like shell shock. As if the mere mentioning of his name resurrected old bones that had been long since buried. Like any child, she had questions about her daddy. Who was he? Where was he? How come he never visits? Kosha learned when she was five that her daddy was dead. That was around the same time her sister Saffron was born. Saffron's daddy immediately became her daddy.

"You know this crazy Charles person?" Kosha asked using air quotes.

She looked from Sage to Cinnamon, who both looked at each other and said nothing. Cat had their tongues but she could tell they knew something about this man who caused everyone in the room to gasp for air. Cinnamon shrugged and placed a set of earbuds in her ear. She turned up her music, drowning out the Maury Povich moment. According to her mother, and what she'd heard her father mention over the years, crazy Charles was indeed the father. Cinnamon didn't mean to appear heartless, but she had bigger issues on the horizon with that fool Mitch.

"Look, I know crazy... I mean... I know Charles from around my neighborhood, but I didn't know he was your pops. I swear," Sage said holding her right hand over her heart.

"Well, that has yet to be proven," Saffron chimed in.

"I think mother's violent response to the accusation is all the validity we need at this point."

"It doesn't even matter. You're damn near thirty."

"Says a person who has always known the truth about her biological father."

Saffron looked up from her phone.

"I'm sorry Kosha. I didn't mean it like that."

She never meant to make her sister feel inadequate, especially not now. She could show a little more empathy, as this man Charles could potentially be the missing link to her sisters' life. It suddenly hit her like a ton of bricks. What if Kosha had other siblings, perhaps a sister on her dads' side that she liked more? Saffron started to panic. Her mother needed to fix this and fix it quick.

The front door swung open and slammed shut. In walked Cayenne fuming. Right behind her was Mitch pleading for her to slow down. He tried grabbing for her arm, but she yanked away. Cinnamon jumped to her feet, followed by Sage. Kosha was too busy in her own world to even realize the commotion. She had a whole family someplace out there. This new reality created welcoming butterflies, as

Saffron selfishly sat toying with the idea of someone replacing her. Mitch cooled his heels as he noticed Cinnamon approaching the scene.

"Aunt Cayenne, what happened?" Cinnamon flat out asked, skipping the pleasantries. She swiftly moved pass Mitch, shoulder bumping him in the process. Sage kept a close eye on Mitch, daring him to react. It wouldn't be their first brawl with a member of the opposite sex. Cinnamon often hung with the boys, climbing trees, playing baseball and tackling them during flag football. Bad sportsmanship caused a few boys to talk mess off the field, which resulted in Cinnamon slap boxing them into saying "uncle". Sage recalled a handful of times where she had to jump in, but her sister usually handled herself well.

"I'm okay."

"You're not," Sage said passing her aunty several Kleenex. Her eyeliner had begun to run down her cheeks. Her makeup now streaked. Her eyes were red and full of sadness. Sage rubbed her back as she sobbed into the tissue. Cinnamon tightened her fist. She was ready to put paws on Mitch, especially after their encounter this morning.

"Just tell me the truth. Who is she?"

Mitch kneeled to her side. "There is no one else. I love you."

"Then why all the secret calls and texts? Just tell me the truth, Mitch."

"Baby, you're my only one. I promise."

"You've been glued to that stupid phone for weeks, months."

"It's all business."

"So why the hell is your call log empty? There's no text history?"

Mitch looked dumbfounded.

"What happened to the text you received just before we left Manhattan yesterday?"

Mitch tried his best not to look in Cayenne's direction.

"You paid the cable bill, car insurance and spoke to your parents in Arizona twice. Now your phone is suddenly wiped clean. All communication has vanished. Are you fucking Houdini?"

"Wait, you went through my phone?" Mitch asked rather surprised.

Cayenne looked embarrassed for snooping. She never wanted to be that kind of girl who couldn't trust her man. She would rather break things off before spying on him. She usually trusted her gut, and her gut told her Mitch wasn't exactly being forthcoming. His skittish behavior had her concerned that he was seeing someone.

"Yes, I went through your phone. I'm not proud of it, but I did it. Lately, I've been questioning your loyalty to me, to this relationship."

"Honey, can we talk about this in private?"

Not only was Sage and Cinnamon standing guard, but Mr. Brown and Coriander had returned from their long walk on the property. The spotlight was now on Mitch, and not in a good way.

"What's going on in here?" Clifford asked peeling off his winter coat.

"Mr. Brown, it's a huge misunderstanding."

Clifford's eyebrow arched up, and his lips twisted. There was always something strange about Mitch. He never fully liked or approved of the man but he tried to remain neutral with who his daughters decided to date.

"Oh, daddy!"

Cayenne fell into her daddy's arms, sobbing like a four-year-old child.

"What the hell did you do to my daughter?"

"Nothing, Sir. It's just a miscommunication."

Clifford walked Cayenne into his study and closed the door. Everyone knew to find a corner and duck because there was no telling what Grandpa Cliff would be totting when he returned. Cayenne was his little firecracker, and also his favorite. As everyone dispersed, Cinnamon stayed seated whistling a tune of death.

"You think this is a joke?"

She shrugged. "Who am I to pass up a good laugh?"

"Your aunt believes I'm screwing around on her. I would never."

"Hate to break it to you buddy, but technically you are. It might not be with another female, but you're messing around with that illegal."

"Illegal that I buy from you," he whispered.

"Hey, everyone knows I'm street affiliated. I own my truth."

Mitch grabbed a beer from the fridge, twisted the cap. He took a swig and laughed.

"You know, you're a piece of work. "

"I've been called worse."

"No, seriously how do you do it?"

"I don't know what you mean."

He took another swig, belched.

"I figured I would be the least of your concerns, especially with the Dread toe-tagged at the city morgue."

Oh shit! The Dread is dead? How could he possibly know this? Cinnamon thought as her heart pounded in her chest.

"I'm sorry, who?"

"You, your man Ra-San..." he whistled the same tune of death and shook his head.

"Don't look shocked. I know people."

Tiny beads of sweat formed on her brow.

"Nah son you got me confused."

"Don't bullshit me. We're practically family now. Word is the Dread is sitting on ice."

Cinnamon's poker face disappeared. She suddenly looked sick. If the Dread was dead, then that meant she was in deep trouble. Mitch read her thoughts, opened the fridge and slid a cold one across the granite countertop.

"You and your man are wanted in connection of a murder. If I were you, I'd stay the fuck out my business and get yourself a lawyer."

CHAPTER 10

The long walk and talk with her daddy did some good, but Coriander needed a professional. Daddy's love was essential, but she needed someone to give it to her straight, no chaser. Corianders therapist, Ms. Ann wasn't available for consult. She was vacationing with her loved ones in Dubai for the holidays. Coriander wished she would have opted out and taken her daughters on an extravagant getaway. A private villa in Saint Tropez would have been lovely. A tropical mountainside hideaway in Costa Rica with panoramic views would have been exquisite. Instead, she was subjected to her drunken sister-in-law drudging up old bones.

No matter how far you go in life there's always somebody to remind you of what you use to do. Simone would never let her forget her past. Coriander thought of paying someone to bury her a long time ago, but realize that would only break her brother Bay's heart. Now faced with the daunting task of explaining to her grown-ass-daughter who her biological father was, gave her some serious heartburn.

"I owe you both an apology. My behavior today was despicable. I'm embarrassed because I let that..." Coriander chewed her bottom lip. "I allowed someone to take control of my emotions. In life, people will do and say all sorts of thing, and that's their prerogative. It's about how you choose to respond. My response was appalling, to say the least."

"Momma, she got what she deserved," Saffron said.

"Well, if that's true then baby I deserve far worse. My past is not pretty, and I've never once tried to pretend like it was. I've tried to always remain an open book."

"Not always," Kosha chimed in.

Corianders eyes hit the floor, too ashamed to look Kosha in the face. She was correct. All the war stories, adventures, and journeys she'd share over the years never once included who her biological father was. She never even knew his name.

"You said he was dead."

"He was, to me."

"That's incredibly selfish, don't you think?"

"Yes, but I had my reasons."

Kosha folded her arms across her chest and waited for her mother to explain.

Coriander actually didn't know where to start. After a long pause, Kosha stood to her feet.

"Either you tell me or I can get Aunt Simone's version of what happened? I'm sure she would be thrilled to rewind the tape from the beginning."

"Rewinding the tape from the beginning won't be necessary. Simone was around, but she can't tell you *my* story, because it's not hers to tell. I'm willing to share with you what you need to know, but don't you ever threaten to go over my head on anything."

The look in her mother's eyes told her to pipe down. After witnessing what happened to the last girl, Kosha made a mental note to tread lightly.

"Charles Sullivan is his name. He lived across the hall from us. Your uncle Bay and Charles were childhood best friends. Those two were thick as thieves. Charles was just a nappy head scruffy kid who played basketball from the time the sun came up, till it went down. He wasn't all that good, but he was tall so that counted for something. Aside from being a half-ass ball player that man sure could sing. He had an unbelievable voice. Anyway, Charles lived with his mom and five sisters. His dad, Mr. Otis was serving time for a bank robbery. Ms. Catherine did her best raising six kids, but her best usually meant Charles went without."

"I have a grandmother, five aunties and a grandfather who served time?"

"Unfortunately, Ms. Catherine passed away before you were born. Last I heard, Mr. Otis suffers from dementia and lives with one of the sisters."

"Damn, that's crazy," Saffron said.

"It was the dead of winter when my daddy brought home the keys to our new home. We were so excited to finally be moving on up like the Jefferson's. I remember that day like it was yesterday. Charles helped Bay and I pack dishes, clothes and haul boxes down several flights of steps. That cold winter day was the last time anyone saw Charles. By summer, Charles had reinvented himself and was now going by the name Sully. His name was ringing bells throughout all five boroughs."

"As in he turned to dealing?" Kosha asked.

Saffron sucked her teeth. "Come on Harvard, you really need clarification on that?"

"That's putting it lightly, but yes. Sully was the man. He was no longer the nappy headed lanky kid with the busted shoes and faded clothes."

Coriander smiled. "All the girls wanted him. Sully was tall, light skin, broad shoulders and had the cutest pudgy nose."

Kosha rubbed her nose. She always questioned where she got her features. *I must get my height from my daddy,* she thought. Her mother and Saffron were barely five-foot-five, while she was five-eight in flats.

"Simone says I'm a gold digger... but hey, you know the rest of that song. I can't lie. I was attracted to his come up. He had respect in the streets, which gave me power. Your dad and I quickly became a thing. I benefited tremendously because I was Sully's girl."

"Did you love him?"

Coriander smiled. "I did."

"What changed?"

"Everything changed."

Corianders eyes watered.

"It was the Fourth of July weekend, and Sully wanted to do it up big. He rented a house for all his crew to come and hang out at Jones Beach. In typical Sully style, he paid for everything. Those invited, invited others and before long there were well over a hundred people at this party. An altercation broke out and shots were fired. Everyone scattered and ducked for cover. Unfortunately, Sully's baby sister was hit, and was pronounced dead on the scene."

Both Saffron and Kosha gasped.

"We had no idea she was even at the party. There were so many people there."

"That's so sad," Kosha said.

"Ms. Catherine suffered a fatal heart attack shortly after the funeral. Your dad couldn't deal, so he started getting high. He started lacing his weed with coke. It was rumored that he was using heroin but I never personally witnessed it. I tried talking to him and begged him to get some help. He stopped listening to me. He barely knew I was in the room half the time. Sully's behavior became more erratic and I was honestly in fear of my life."

"Did he hurt you?" Saffron asked.

"Not physically, but we argued a lot. He threatened to put a bullet between my eyes once. It was at that moment I knew I had to escape him. I called your uncle Bay over to our apartment one day when Sully was out of town. I had two large suitcases; both were filled to the rim with Sully's money. They were too heavy for me to carry alone."

Coriander took a sip of water.

"I took it all, the money and the jewelry. Your uncle had no idea what was in the suitcases. Sully came looking for me a few days later, but I was long gone."

"Where did you go?" Kosha asked.

"I jumped in my car and drove to California. My past was finally in my rearview. It didn't take me long to find a reasonably priced studio apartment. I was there all of two weeks when I found out I was pregnant with you."

"For the first time in my life, I was afraid. Here I am in LA, with no family, no connections and pregnant. I called home and heard that Sully's sisters had committed him to Bellevue for psychiatric evaluation. No one knew I was pregnant. Your grandma came to visit nine months later and there you were. Just a few weeks old and you were already trying to talk and hold your head up."

"Does my father even know I exist?"

"Simone, of course, blabbed her mouth to anyone who would listen. Sully's sister heard about you and told him. By this time your father was several cans short of a six-pack and a crack head. I heard he was sleeping in abandon buildings and begging for money to score. So you understand why I had to keep moving? There was no way I could turn back."

***

Bay emptied BC powder into his mouth and took a swig of water. A pack of frozen peas provided some relief to his jaw, but his ears were being tortured by Simone's nonstop rant. Cori this, and Cori that. He wished she would just shut the hell up and take a nap. For someone who just got the life almost choked out of them, she sure had a lot to say. Bay massaged his jaw, and couldn't help but laugh to himself. His sister socked him good.

"What's so damn funny?"

"Nothing."

"It's something. Go ahead and share."

Bay plopped down on the edge of the bed and removed his socks and shoes. The BC powder was fast acting, and all he wanted to do was sleep.

"Come to bed."

"I'm ready to go."

"Don't be ridiculous. Come to bed."

Bay propped a stack of pillows behind his head and yarned.

"I'm serious. Let's get out of here."

Bay closed his eyes and before long he was snoring. Simone stomped her way to the adjoined bathroom, filled a glass with water. She called his name several times before splashing his face. Bay jumped up in a fit of rage.

"Are you crazy?"

Simone folded her arms across her chest.

"I told you I'm ready to leave."

"Then go!"

She was shocked. "What do you mean, go?"

"I'm so tired of you. All you do is complain and I'm sick of it. If you're so unhappy with me then just leave. I can't handle this madness any longer. You drink too much Simone. Your hatred for my sister has become an obsession."

"It was our tee-shirt business. That snake cut me out, left me in the projects while she went to LA and became a big shot A-listed designer."

"Simone, my sister has paid you back countless times. She has done more for this family then required." Bay winced the moment he said it. Corianders help was to remain anonymous. He knew his wife would never openly accept what she would perceive as charity.

"Come again," Simone said tapping her foot against the floor. When he didn't respond she threw a shoe at him.

"What do you mean she's paid me back? What has that whore ever done for me and my family?"

Bay angrily snatched off his wet clothes and slid into a pair of sweatpants and dry tee-shirt. He was beyond pissed at his wife.

"Listen, I tried to be a supportive husband. I was your number one cheerleader. You had a brilliant mind, and I knew for sure you would have your own successful business up and running in no time. I've taken out countless student loans on your behalf because I knew how important education was to you."

"Bay, I appreciate all of that but answer my question. How has Cori paid me back?"

"You went into finance and accounting, then marketing and advertisement and several other areas of study. You earned two masters degrees and just last week you told me you want to pursue your doctorate degree."

"*So*, I want my PhD!"

"So, the cost for your love of academia grows daily. I owed well over one million in federal student loans. This debt is the reason we've never owned a home. I've worked check to check my entire life, and I have nothing to show for it."

The tears in her husband's eyes didn't move her one bit. It was his job to invest in her happiness. What did he expect for her to do, kiss his feet?

"You said owed, as in past tense."

"Wow, have you heard anything else I just said?"

"I'm more interested in learning how Cori has paid me back."

"Okay, you really want to know?"

"Yes, enlighten me."

"As an early retirement gift, Cori offered to pay off all of my debts including *your* student loans and I accepted."

"Wait, what?"

"For years Cori has offered to help us, but I said no out of respect for you and your damn feelings. My parents have offered to buy us a nice home, but you let your pride get in the way. I've invested in you because I love you."

Simone had to take a seat and catch her breath. She couldn't believe her husband actually allowed Coriander to wipe his debts clean. She had to admit, her student loans were out of control. Bay owed fifty thousand in credit card debt, and they had old medical expenses from back in the day. Usually, her house phone would ring ten times a day from a different creditor looking for blood. She noticed the calls had stopped all together over a month ago. A sinister smile crept across her face.

"Tell Cori you need five million dollars."

Bay's eyes were as large as dinner plates.

"Have you lost your damn mind, Simone?"

She stood to her feet and began to pace the room like an evil genius.

"I'll obtain a lawyer to argue the fact that Cori agreed to *finally* pay me intellectual rights on our tee-shirt designs. We agreed on seven million, which she paid a portion directly to my student loans, charged-off credit cards, and hospital bills. The attorney will argue that Cori suddenly changed her mind about paying the remaining balance."

"Over my dead body." Bay gritted his teeth.

Simone motioned her way towards the large window, which had a view of the lake. She wondered if five million was a low ball amount. The rule of thumb was to always ask for more than you actually wanted. She decided ten million would suffice. After lawyer's fees, she figured she would be left with around seven million. She held her hands to her mouth.

"Holy cow, this could work."

Simone looked over her shoulder for Bay, but he was long gone.

CHAPTER 11

Clifford found Rosemary in the lounge shuffling through old boxes. There on the floor, she sat, surrounded by old vinyl records and crumbled sheet music. She glanced up at him, smiled. He cracked one back at her and released a sigh of relief. The footprint of their home proved to be a lot larger that day, as he searched high and low for his wife. He last spotted her in bed with a cup of peppermint tea to soothe her nerves.

"There you are. I've been looking all over the place for you."

"Couldn't sleep," she said shuffling through oldies but goodies. Al Green, Aretha Franklin, Diana Ross, Barry White, and BB King Records sprawled before her.

"I've been looking for my Christmas sheet music. It was here yesterday. Maybe Catherine moved it when she was cleaning. I sure would hate to call her, but I really need it."

"Please don't call Catherine. I'm so embarrassed Alberto had to witness the reckless behavior. It's a crying shame."

"They probably think our kids have no home training."

"Come now woman, get off that floor before you break something that can't be fixed."

"Oh, I'll be just fine," she swatted his hand away.

"Why are you looking for sheet music?"

Rosemary peeked over the top of her readers.

"I figured I'll get the family together and we could sing Christmas Carols here in the lounge. Perhaps we could do Karaoke. What better way to pour some joy back into this weekend? Mark my words, music is the bridge to love."

"Hum, well..." Clifford paused

"What happened now?"

Clifford took a seat behind the baby grand piano. He played a few keys and then stopped. He wasn't much of the pianist like his wife. Rosemary was a self-taught professional in her own right. When her fingers graced the keys, the most harmonious music was made.

"Cliff, don't beat around the bush. What happened?"

Clifford went to help Rosemary as she struggled to get off the floor. He held both of her hands. She was such a sweet lady who asked for very little of anyone. All she wanted was a peaceful holiday weekend with the people she loved the most. *Those selfish MoFo's*, Clifford thought. Rosemary sat down behind the piano. His Dear wife was so optimistic. She was certain she could soften the hearts of her children with just a few keystrokes.

"It's just that I don't think music is enough to save this weekend. I know you had your heart set on mending this family, but there are some serious unresolved issues going on. Now, I tried to manage the chaos as best possible but them Negro's are getting on my last damn nerve."

Rosemary chuckled.

"Be strong babe. Don't give up on them just yet. The lord has a way of working things out for the good. He knows how to make a way out of no way. He can suddenly shift the minds and hearts of those crazy kids just like that." Rosemary snapped her fingers.

"Darling, that's a whole lot of ego and stubbornness going on out there. I don't doubt what you're saying but the lord better come quick because Bay just tossed Simone's luggage out the front door."

"Where are Cori and her girls?"

"They appear to be fine now. I'm flying by the seat of my pants around here. As I said, black Jesus better come quick."

All of a sudden Rosemary seemed blasé about the recent reporting's. Now realizing her reaction to the drama from the beginning should have been to walk in love. She allowed the current climate to shift her emotions. Like some weak punk, she decided to crawl into bed with wet eyes and a broken heart. The Lord's voice boomed in her ears and his words rocked her spirit. *Bridge the gap* is what she heard loud and clear. She was strong, she was a warrior, and there would be a cold day in hell before she allowed her family to subscribe to discord.

"Woman, did you hear anything I just said? Bay is tossing Simone's luggage onto the front the porch."

Rosemary chuckled again. This time Clifford joined in.

"I sure do have to admit it's about damn time that boy grew a pair. Ever since he was a teen he'd been chasing after that Looney Tune. Don't get me wrong, I love my daughter-in-law but she's a handful," said Clifford.

"I wonder what's gotten into him. Maybe it has something to do with the fight from earlier?"

"Probably so," Clifford said taking a deep breath.

"Don't worry babe. I've got this. I'll set them all straight soon enough."

"Better be sooner than later cause there's serious trouble brewing with Cayenne and Mitch as well. I just don't understand that boy. There's something very strange about him. Just can't seem to put my finger on it. My Firecracker feels the same way, at least there's some recent suspicion on whether or not he's sniffing around some other lady's skirt."

"That's not it. Mitch is old faithful, but not completely forthcoming with his recent extracurricular activities. I'll agree that boy has some serious issues, but he loves the ground Cayenne walks on."

Clifford squinted his eyes at Rosemary. His wife meditated daily and had a direct connection to the lord. It was like she picked up the telephone and called her best friend for the daily news. She knew where to go to seek resolution for all things concerning her and her family. Although Rosemary knew many things, she never misused or abused her Intel. Only when instructed by the Lord did his jump in to provide counsel.

"Let me guess, the Lord has given you step by step instructions on how to save Christmas."

"Christmas doesn't need saving," she smiled while patting his hand.

"Do me a favor and go round up the troops. I want everyone in this room, stat. Tell them I said so!"

Moments later the family trickled in one by one. Some took a seat on the large sectional; others found oversized cushy bean bags to cuddle with. Clifford pulled the French doors shut as he was the last one in.

Rosemary sat behind the piano and played the most delightful music. Melodic tunes soothed their minds as they patiently waited for mother matriarch to speak. Her eyes bounced from each face and no one seemed happy.

"Depression, Pain, Guilt, Selfishness, Disrespect is all I see right now."

Everyone chimed in at the same time. Rosemary looked towards her husband and nodded her head. A sharp whistle escaped his lips and the room fell silent.

"A house divided cannot stand. It's time to dissolve the hate. Now you damn kids have been bumping your gums for the last two days. My wife has something important to say. You will let her speak without interruptions. Do I make myself clear?"

Rosemary could always count on her husband for crowd control. She thanked him.

"This weekend was for us to fellowship with one another, join hands and break bread together. All I've seen is ego, envy and no empathy for what the next person may be going through. We go all year long harboring old feelings instead of picking up a phone to work it out."

Rosemary's fingertips danced across the keys with grace. Each stoke was precise and deliberate. The beautiful music came to a halt as she rose from the piano.

"There's a spirit of divisiveness that cloaks this family. I'm here to proclaim the devil is a liar. No weapon formed amongst this family shall prosper. We may quarrel, we may have a difference of opinion, and we all have different lenses from which we view the world. No one here is authorized to pass judgment on the next. I mean no one."

"Amen," Clifford chimed in.

"The backbiting, jealousy, envy, and strife amongst you all is destroying this family. Your hatred is poisoning our bloodline. Unresolved issues only fester and grow and guess what? When you go home to see the lord, your offspring's continue your legacy. This is how wars are started. Family rivalries begin through ancestral hate for one another."

Rosemary held back her tears. She had to be strong.

"Sure, we fight, we complain about this and that and everything beneath the sun but despite it all we're family. We stick together through the good, the bad and the ugly. In the last two days, I've seen the devil run rampant. Guess what, the devil ain't welcomed here."

"Hum, I know that's right!" Clifford said clapping his hands. Rosemary looked over at her husband and smiled. She loved that man so much.

"So, with all that said there are obviously a lot of unresolved issues we need to address. I propose that each of you come to the center of the floor and express how you feel, respectfully of course. Let's cut the snakes head off and end this toxic cycle. Otherwise, we can't grow."

Rosemary scanned the faces of her loved ones again, and there wasn't a dry eye in the room. She waited for a volunteer, but no one budged. Rosemary knew this was a well defining moment, which could make or break them as a unit. She closed her eyes and prayed for someone to be brave enough to step forward. Clifford approached his wife, grabbed and kissed the back of her hand.

"We can't make them participate."

As Clifford led saddened Rosemary back to the piano to sit, Mitch stood up.

"I know I'm not officially family yet, but something in my spirit is nudging me to speak."

Mitch took to the center of the room and clinched his fist tightly. He was sweating profusely.

"I'm nervous right now. What I'm about to say could make you all look at me differently, but I don't care at this point."

He looked in Cayenne's direction.

"Baby, there is no one else but you. I love you, but ever since my slip and fall accident I've been addicted to painkillers. My doctor refused to renew my prescription and cut me off months ago," Mitch said looking at Cinnamon then back to the love of his life.

"A source from the streets have been supplying me with Oxy and Vicodin. The person I've been texting and calling is... " he swallowed hard. Mitch realized outing Cinnamon would only cause more pain for the Browns. Besides, Cinnamon had to answer to the Lord for her own actions.

"I've been texting and calling my dealer."

"I don't understand," Cayenne said with tears streaming her face.

Mitch ran towards Cayenne and collapsed to her feet.

In a trembling voice, he said "I'm getting help the moment we get back home. I'm so sorry for disappointing you. Please don't leave me."

Rosemary applauded Mitch for being courageous. That wasn't the easiest thing to do, but he took a chance. His public display of bravery was infectious as Cinnamon stood next, and made her way towards the center of the room.

"I'm already known as the wild one. I predict there's not much I can say or do, that will shock any of you at this point."

Crickets.

"Okay, well your assumptions of me are accurate. I'm gay, and no it's not a phase. I'm a high school dropout, never liked school. I like to smoke weed. In fact, I'm high right now. Sarcasm is my middle name. I'm addicted to fast money and fast cars. I'm super smart, I'm thoughtful, caring and I look out for the people I love. I'm coming to you all because I need help." Her voice cracked. She fanned her face, trying hard to prevent her tears from falling.

"I'm in some serious trouble back home and I'm scared."

Bay jumped to his feet, "What kind of trouble?"

"Daddy, somebody got killed and the police want me for questioning."

The whole room gasped in disbelief.

"I knew this would happen. Dammit Cinnamon, I told you to stay out those streets, take your ass back to school and be somebody. Now you're wanted for murder?"

"No, I didn't kill anyone"

"Daddy, it wasn't her fault," Sage chimed in.

Cinnamon trembled not in fear of her father, but in fear of being locked in prison for the rest of her natural born life. Crooked cops had a way of twisting the truth.

"Son, now is not the time to pass judgment on her."

"Pops, you don't understand. This girl has been a thorn in my side for years."

"Don't talk about my child like that," Simone jumped to Cinnamons defense.

If looks could kill, Simone would be dead. Bay had thrown her belongings out like day old trash and was seconds from tossing her along with it. If it hadn't been for her daughters coming to her defense, she would be frozen like a Popsicle somewhere in the middle of Roxbury.

"If it weren't for the main roads being covered in ice and snow, your ass would have been on the next Greyhound smoking."

Bay turned back to his daughter who was now in tears.

"I'm here for you. It's going to be alright."

Rosemary held her hand out. "Come here, child."

Cinnamon sat next to her grandma and cried hard.

"You know, the Lord has placed each of us on this earth for a reason."

"Yes ma'am, I do."

"Are you ready to discover your purpose?"

Cinnamon could barely speak. Her voice arrested in fear of what would happen the moment she stepped foot back on the block. The Dreads people would be looking for her and payback was a bitch.

"Yes ma'am, I am. I'm ready to change."

"Then you will stay here in Roxbury with us. We will hire the best lawyer to fight this."

"That's right baby girl. We're family and we stick together," Clifford said wiping away his own tears.

Without protest Cinnamon agreed. Sage joined her sister, embracing her with a loving hug. The truth was out and now her sister could finally start the healing process. She felt a sense of peace knowing Cinnamon would stay with her grandparents. Sage could now go off to Spelman and continue her education without worry. Sage spoke a few words of gratitude. Next Bay thanked his parents for offering the support. Even Simone added her two cents of appreciation.

With their arms linked to one another Coriander and her two daughters made their way towards the center of the room. Kosha stood on the right, Saffron on the left and Coriander was in the middle. Their stance exhibited unbreakable strength and unconditional love.

"Mommy, daddy... I'm sorry for my behavior this weekend. Although provoked, I should have never acted in such a savage manner. You raised me better than that. My dirty laundry was aired, and I'm glad it was."

Coriander looked in Simone's direction.

"My daughter now knows the truth about her father. Thank you so much."

Simone felt small and wanted to magically disappear.

"Charles Sully is my baby daddy."

Coriander kissed Kosha on the cheek.

"Many moons ago, I did love your father and he loved me. You were a love child, not a mistake. If and when you're ready, I'm willing to introduce you to your other side."

Kosha pulled in a lung full of air, nodded as she was speechless.

"While I have your attention, I wanted to inform you all that I'm stepping down from Troos."

Simone's mouth dropped to the floor. She caught a glimpse of her husband Bay grinning like a Cheshire cat. She wondered if he spoke a word of her diabolical plan to funnel cash. She felt a pain in the pit of her stomach, realizing she'd hated Coriander all these eyes for the very thing she was attempting to do. *Two wrongs don't make a right*, she thought wringing her hands together in shame. Besides, now that their debts were cleared Simone figured she and Bay could now own a piece of parcel of their own.

"Why are you stepping down?" Sage asked.

"Personal reasons that I will make public soon enough. Don't worry Sage; your Atlanta internship with Troos Couture is still intact."

"Are you sick child?"

"No, daddy I'm not sick. I promise I'm healthy as an Ox."

"Then what is it?"

"Daddy, trust me. We will have an opportunity to discuss in further detail, privately."

Clifford grabbed a seat. Confessionals had proven to be too much to handle all at once. Murder, sexuality, drug usage, infidelity, DNA and company restructures caused him to pour a glass of cognac.

CHAPTER 12

It was Christmas morning and the Brown's were all gathered around the tree. As usual, Rosemary instructed everyone to wear Santa hats, and matching red onesies. Shockingly there were no complaints from anyone, not even Saffron. In fact, she embraced her grandma's wardrobe selection as fun and festive.

It was gift giving time. Grandpa Clifford started with the larger packages and then worked his way down to the smallest of the presents. Rosemary's heart was full, as she watched everyone's face light up with joy. With the help of online shopping, she had managed to order the latest and greatest tech gadgets for the young ones. She figured the adults could all use cozy robes and slippers with their initials inscribed. She also gifted body butter, scented candles, and essential oils to everyone.

Sage squealed. "Oh grandma, grandpa, you're the best ever!"

She received a laptop loaded with all the latest software imaginable. She also received a highly sophisticated camera to capture her college journey. She was forever grateful to her grandparents.

"Ooh momma, this body butter smells amazing," Cayenne said rubbing a considerable amount into the palms of her hand.

"Ms. Rosie, this essential oil smells divine," said Simone.

"Well thank you. The body butter, essential oil and that peppermint tea you're sipping on are all a part of my new line of products."

"What you talking about momma?" Coriander asked, dipping her finger into Cayenne's jar.

"Ouch! Heffa you scratched me."

"Keep your nasty hands out my jar," Cayenne smiled and stuck out her tongue.

"You girls behave, there's enough to go around. I wanted it to be a surprise."

"Your mother has been working on this idea for two years now. Her products are all natural, plant-based ingredients. In fact, she has sourced ninety percent of ingredients straight from our property."

"Grandma, let me find out you a boss around here," Cinnamon said taking a whiff of the peppermint oil which immediately opened her nasal passage.

"Yes, indeed I am. Now that you will be here full time I can certainly use your help. The goal is to harvest and incorporate my herbs and organically grown plants into all natural everyday products. It's all about clean, chemical-free living."

"I'm here to serve you in whatever capacity. I'm honored." Cinnamon said with tears in her eyes.

"Mitch, I see you've got your new beard and all. You must try my conditioner. It's a miracle in a bottle. It softens hydrates and moisturizes. It's a product dedicated to men," Rosemary shamelessly plugged.

"Dang momma that sounded like a professional commercial" Bay said clapping.

"I've been practicing. This old lady still got some living to do."

"That's right grandma," both Saffron and Kosha said at the same time.

"Anyways, enough about me. Let's get this party started. Bay and Mitch get more wood for the fire. Kosha, Saffron, Cinnamon, and Sage you girls bring the pies and cakes out. Simone, grab some dishes and silverware. Cayenne, Cori... grab the Cognac!"

Rosemary and Clifford's fingers interlocked as they snuggled on the loveseat. They were tickled pink watching everyone scramble in all directions. The Browns were finally working together as a family unit. The moment was priceless, precious and perfect.

"Crisis averted," Clifford whispered.

"Thank the Lord. *Hallelujah*" said Rosemary.

"I was thinking we should get together for New Year's Eve. I'm sure Cori wouldn't mind us all crashing her Manhattan pint house to see the Apple drop."

Clifford gave Rosemary a stern look.

"What, too soon?"

Each book from **The Brown Family series** is a standalone novella, and can be read in any order. Pick one and enjoy. Happy Reading!!!

ABOUT THE AUTHOR

LaQuarn Michaels is an Author of Urban Fiction Drama, Romantic Suspense, Erotica Fiction and a flock of draw dropping short stories. Her gift for writing has been known to establish a personal connection with the reader from page one. Her style of writing constantly delivers tantalizing twisted plots, and unforgettable characters.

When she is not reading or writing her next bestseller, she is spending time with her husband and children soaking up sun on a sandy beach. She's a fan of domestic and international travels, amazing cuisine and good vibes. LaQuarn Michaels is a native New Yorker, born and raised in South Jamaica Queens. She now resides in Atlanta, GA.

www.laquarnmichaels.com